LOVE IN
THE DAYS
OF RAGE

Also by Lawrence Ferlinghetti

A Coney Island of the Mind
After the Cries of the Birds
Endless Life: Selected Poems
Her
Inside the Trojan Horse
Landscapes of Living and Dying
Leaves of Life: Fifty Drawings from the Model
The Mexican Night: Travel Journal
Moscow in the Wilderness, Segovia in the Snow
European Poems & Transitions:
Over All the Obscene Boundaries
Paroles by Jacques Prévert (translation)
Pictures of the Gone World
The Populist Manifestos
Routines
The Secret Meaning of Things
Seven Days in Nicaragua Libre
Starting from San Francisco
A Trip to Italy and France
Tyrannus Nix?
Unfair Arguments with Existence
Who Are We Now?

LOVE IN THE DAYS OF RAGE

LAWRENCE FERLINGHETTI

THE OVERLOOK PRESS

WOODSTOCK & NEW YORK

This paperback edition first published in the United States in 2001 by
The Overlook Press, Peter Mayer Publishers, Inc.
Woodstock & New York

WOODSTOCK:
One Overlook Drive
Woodstock, NY 12498
www.overlookpress.com
[for individual orders, bulk and special sales, contact our Woodstock office]

NEW YORK:
141 Wooster Street
New York, NY 10012

Library of Congress Cataloging-in-Publication Data

Ferlinghetti, Lawrence.
Love in the days of rage / Lawrence Ferlinghetti.
p. cm.
I. Title.
PS3511.E557L59 1988   813'.54   88-3589

Printed in Canada
ISBN 1-58567-202-5
1 3 5 7 9 8 6 4 2

for
Fernando Pessoa
whose Anarchist Banker
prefigured mine

LOVE IN THE DAYS OF RAGE

■ | □

The last time she saw Paris when last the sweet birds sang was from a fast train heading south in 1968 at the time of the student revolution, and it was almost the last train to get out, but that is getting ahead of the story, which began late one evening at the Coupole in Montparnasse when someone introduced her to Julian Mendes, and thereby hangs a tale of love in those days of rage. It was some time before she saw him again, having a late supper by himself in the back of the Coupole. At first she took him for a Spaniard or a Basque, although she could not have said exactly why. There was something of the mountains about him, with his head that looked as if it had been cut from rock, almost ugly in profile, but with a fierce charm, with a very small scar on one cheek, and he rather formally dressed as if he belonged to some former age or at least as if he purchased his suits in foreign capitals. He definitely didn't look very French. He was perhaps fifty-five, and she was certainly fascinated by him yet at the same time a bit wary, for there was something about him, a look in his eye, a curious reserve or distance, something unfathomable and withdrawn, so that she kept her distance whenever she happened to see him either in the Coupole or at some art opening or in the lobby of a movie, always by himself. Her private life was complicated enough that year, she had more than enough men to keep her occupied when she wasn't working, and she enjoyed living by herself, having freed herself from an unlikely liaison earlier that year, her fortieth year in fact, with all the pent-up passions of that age.

■ 2 □

His name had a warmth and elegance about it that she liked, the decadent elegance of characters in pre–World War One novels like Briffault's *Europa,* that seemed to sum up a dying culture and that Annie had come across in George Whitman's bookstore down in the Rue de la Bûcherie. And then one morning she ran into Julian Mendes coming out of the Métro at Odéon, and he remembered her name right off, and they sat down together on the terrace of the Café Mabillon close by and ordered coffee and sat drinking it and talking about nothing, almost as if they had always been together. She felt some instant affinity with him, almost as if she had known him for a long time in some other life in another country, which of course could not be, since France was the only country

outside America she'd ever seen. She liked the way he
talked, and she agreed to go to a movie with him another evening, and then after the movie they went to the
Mabillon and sat there for a long time late in the evening watching the crowds go by and talking. There was
a kind of force in his thinking, indeed a passion, in the
flow of his thought, which struck her especially whenever they got on politics, which was an unavoidable subject those days, especially around the Sorbonne, which
was just up the street. And when they got up to leave
the Mabillon that night it was almost midnight and the
terrace was deserted except for the fat figure of a man
at a table at the far end of the terrace, almost in the
street. It was "Duke" McIntyre, the famous American
translator, who was a fixture in the Mabillon and seemed
to know everyone who hung out there, a mixture of
expatriates of various sorts and students from the Beaux-
Arts and street artists, as well as a few prostitutes and
their pimps, especially late at night, some of them reg-
ulars at the Pergola across the street, which stayed open
all night loaded with various kinds of hustlers. And it
seemed now that the Duke knew Julian Mendes too, for
he hailed him with a great sweep of his arm and cries
of recognition, grappling for his arm and pressing him
into a seat next to him, all of which Julian Mendes went
along with good-naturedly, for there was nothing for it,
in any case. "Well!" exclaimed the Duke. "If it isn't Se-
ñor Moneybug hisself, caught in the dead of night with
a fetching charmer, indeed!" And he ogled Annie up and
down, seeming overjoyed with what he saw, and he swung
around in his seat, signaling the waiter to bring three
more of what he was drinking, which happened to be
Ricard. Everything about him suggested the nineteen
twenties or thirties, his well-cut suit with the wide la-

pels, his shiny black shoes and his art-deco tie, as well as his tight little Chaplin moustache, which seemed stuck to his florid face. His large gut with the watch chain across it heaved when he spoke, breathing heavily, leaning back with his arms stretched out on neighboring chairs. "Listen to this, will you!" he exclaimed, addressing the empty terrace as if it were a crowd of admirers. "Listen to this. Here I am the last surviving golden tongue of the Lost Generation, the very ghost of Nonstop Fitzgerald or Hairy Crosby himself, here washed up without a sou on the hospitable maw of M'sieur Mabillon, without a sou, I repeat, and along comes the Emperor of the Cult of Lucre himself, genius hero of masterly manipulation, who, if he could manage to manipulate a little lucre onto those little white saucers, we might all relax and enjoy the new millennium. . . ." Julian Mendes paid, and the waiter went away, leaving their Ricards in front of them. Julian Mendes poured a little water into his, and the liquid turned from green to yellowish white. "I see the current king of bohemia is in fine form tonight," said Julian Mendes to the Duke, hoisting his glass to him, who raised his own and swallowed half of it. "Yes, indeed," the Duke resumed, "and if that isn't a perfect example of C. H. Douglas's Social Credit, I have never seen one. Credit, indeed! But it ain't Social Credit, it's bank credit that runs the world the way they want it run. . . . That's what it's all about, ain't it? The boogeymen in the banks create credit, inflate it, sell it, deflate it, buy it, buy and sell wars and nations, buy and sell armies, buy and sell you and me!" He seemed to be addressing Annie now, as she sat back and gave him her shy smile. The Duke drank off the rest of his drink and picked up hers, his watery eyes the color of the Ricard. A dreamy look came into them as he contemplated An-

nie, swaying slightly in his chair, and in a singsong un-
dertone he mouthed lines from T. S. Eliot, "Lady, whose
shrine stands on a promontory . . . pray for all those
who are in ships—" He stopped short, recalling the
presence of Julian Mendes, and turned to him again,
maintaining the singsong tone. "Pray for all those who
are in banks, pray for all those who are in banks, indeed! Usury, age-old, sitteth by my side. In my most need,
to be my guide—" "What *is* all this about banks?" Julian
Mendes asked playfully. "Ah, he plays innocent now, old
King Credit himself!" The Duke rocked back and forth
as he spoke. "Stealing from governments the right to
issue money, and now we can't git it back from them.
'The hand that signed the paper felled a city.' And the
'paper' nothing but paper printed green by banks that
owned the printing presses as well as the rest of the
world, lock stock and bunghole, and all done with mirrors, with green paper they themselves invented in the
first place!" Inside the café there was one table left with
card players, three old men in berets. They drew their
cards and studied their hands as if they were destiny
itself. Annie could see the smoke from their cigarette
butts coiling up under the green light, as in a Van Don-
gen painting, and she thought of how she would get the
color of the green if she were painting it. The true color
of money was something she had never contemplated
before. It threw a slightly new light on Julian Mendes.

■ 3 □

Thus things began between them, and the days ran through the hourglass into March, and after a while it seemed quite natural for him to come up to her place in the Rue Descartes up behind the Panthéon, her little place with its little sunny rooms, and the spring coming on so warm that year when things were heating up at the Sorbonne and at the Beaux-Arts where she taught. It was the first time Annie would have a European lover, even though it was a long time since she had arrived in Paris from New York, with her illusions and her so red hair and her bag full of more paintbrushes and sketchbooks than clothes. In the Lower East Side she had become a somewhat famous painter, first an abstract expressionist, then a figurative painter, following the generation of Motherwell and de Kooning

and Kline. But she had split off from them all and come
to Paris because she had been invited by some enthusi-
asts of her painting who were on the faculty of the Ecole
des Beaux-Arts, and then she stayed on because they
wanted her to and had even given her a studio of her
own at the school, way up under the eaves, a huge space
by Paris standards. She stayed on as in a dream whose
beginning had been forgotten. She felt now almost as if
she could not paint without that special Paris light, that
pearl light, translucent over the grey rooftops, or rather
she felt she might never again paint in that harsh wide-
open "big sky" light of America. Even in New York, in
Manhattan, in the Lower East Side, it was a big sky, a bit
hedged in, not quite the big sky of Out West but still
like a wide-open wide-angle lens, a great unblinking eye
that left no place to find one's private self, in the wide-
open landscape of America, where everything had fallen
out of the canvases and left only empty abstract expressionist open-fields of subjective desolation, where everything had fallen out into the destroyed streets of the
Lower East Side and lay in heaps in the gutters, piles of
mattresses and bedsprings, broken dolls and brassieres,
shattered mirrors and bent bodies in the dirty dawn,
east of Tompkins Square like some bombed-out Dres-
den, laid out in the pulsing light, which was so very
masculine, yes, a light so masculine and young, which
was just the opposite of that pearl grey Paris light, which
was still so feminine, not so aggressive as the American
light and its aggressive New York School of painters,
compared to Paris with its old light, like some old *grande
dame* dozing off in her Beaux-Arts school. Annie had
never been one of those hard-line New Yorkers who
could never live anywhere else. She had always wanted
to escape, and she did, Paris for her a liberation, as for

so many others, and she had stayed on and on—ten years, fifteen years now, and time winging on, while in her painting she was figuratively digging out those lost human bodies, those torn human remains in the gutter, and putting them back in her canvases, breathing life into them again. She loved the human figure, and had too much to say to be a nonobjective painter. But now it was the spring of 1968, and that old dame which was Paris dozing in the late sun was to be thrust into the light of new 1968 realities and the student revolution, the light of percussion grenades with deafening flashes in the night sky over Saint-Michel and Saint-Germain. That had not happened yet, for it was still only late March on a Sunday afternoon with the sun coming in through the double doors open onto her narrow balcony, and Julian Mendes there, looking through some of her art books and reviews piled up on her coffee table. They had been out walking and had stopped at the Brasserie Lipp in Saint-Germain in the middle of the afternoon and sat down on the terrace and had beer and looked inside and recognized Simone de Beauvoir and Jean-Paul Sartre with his thick glasses reading the papers and talking. "When I was a student I used to see them in here, in the Lipp—they lived above the Café Bonaparte in those days, just down there," Julian said, motioning toward the Place of Saint-Germain-des-Près. "And here they are again, and they're having a lot to say about what's happening now. Everything they've been talking about all these years is coming to pass now—although the students these days haven't really read him, and the ones that have probably think he's a bit *épuisé,* if not *dépassé*. . . ." But, Julian said, it was really Albert Camus who had meant so much to him personally. It was Camus whom Julian admired the most, especially his

L'Homme Révolté, or *The Rebel.* "Yes," said Julian, "I guess
I wouldn't be what I am today without that book!" Which
was a surprising thing for a successful banker to say, but
what was more surprising was that he actually professed
to be an anarchist at heart and claimed that he still lived
by anarchist principles. It made her laugh. He didn't laugh.
His voice took on a certain intensity as he turned to her
and said, "Listen, I don't think it's really very radical to
believe in the only way that makes any sense these days.
You know, the whole house of cards, the whole enormous state that's been erected to run everything gets
bigger and bigger, with more and more rules and reg-
ulations for the little man to abide by, his precious little
freedom more and more cut down to size, to fit in, to
fit the machinery, the little cog without which nothing
can function, the billions of little cogs so important to
the working of the monster machine, and woe be to
those who don't stay in place or get out of line, out of
'sync' as you Americans say. The state sold the little man
a bill of goods called the Social Contract, and the state
had to construct a huge Social Lie to support it—" He
stopped short and laughed softly and looked at her, as
Annie was thinking this all sounded like old rads who
were friends of her father when she was growing up.
"Well," he said, sitting back, with a slight laugh, "I can
see I'm going to have to tell you the story of my life so
you can see how I got this way. . . ." "You remind me
of a lot of people already," said Annie. "You've heard it
all somewhere before?" "Not exactly—you might as well
give me the foreign version." "Well," said Julian, "I might
as well begin at the beginning, or near it, when I was in
my twenties, just out of the University of Lisbon. Only
one side of my family was French. My father's family was
Portuguese, and I grew up mostly there, in Portugal, with

side trips to France where all my mother's relatives lived—but anyway, I wasn't much of a student. I rather liked to live the student life, without doing much work, but the students I hung around with were mostly, like myself, poor sons of a defunct nobility, living precariously under Salazar's murderous regime, as all Portugal lived under his thumb. Well, the students I was with were mostly involved in underground groups, little tiny groups or *groupuscules* that really didn't have a chance of doing anything, being so hidden and dispersed and spending most of their time sitting around in hopeless cellars fiddling with their moustaches. But anyway, it was dangerous, you could be caught with some little handbill in your pocket, late at night, by some fascist police patrol in your neighborhood, and the next thing you knew, in a day or two there'd be a knock or two on your door, and you'd simply disappear. It happened to more than a few of my friends. And then it really started, my 'radical' development, that is. For there was a quite well known professor who somehow managed to remain in his university chair, by various subterfuges—a political science professor—and he became my mentor in a way. I used to audit his lectures, and I read all the little pamphlets and broadsides he wrote under various pseudonyms. He was generally a philosophical anarchist, and he believed in what he taught, and taught us to believe. I think he was caught in some web of his own making years later, still under Salazar's dictatorship, and put away. You have no idea how it was under Salazar back then, how it still is, for he's still there, still in power, but not for much longer, before this year is out he'll be gone, finally, you'll see, and the students will have finally done it, there as here. But back then, when Salazar was just getting started, we had the most boring, the most banal

dictatorship in the world. Every cliché about dictator-
ships was truer for Portugal than anywhere else! But no
matter how absolute power is, there's always some corner holding out, silently, secretly, refusing to conform,
and this of course was around the university, at Lisbon
and at Coimbra, for it's always youth who sees most clearly
through the whole sham, the whole lie of it, youth with
its new eyes, and there was fire in the night out in
Coimbra, while in Lisbon we concentrated on sabotage,
whatever we could bring off in our small ways, mostly
against the Catholic Youth groups, who did the dirty work
for the dictatorship around the university, while of course
our real aim was to bring down the whole fascist state.
The Church was of course one of the most important
supporters of the regime, and we pulled off many a dirty
little trick in and out of the churches, but that was kid
stuff, and it was too dangerous anyway. What we needed
to do was attack the black plague itself, Salazar himself,
but how to do that, with his legions of fascist troops
around him? We were powerless but there were millions powerless like us, even poorer and with less rights
than we had, someday they would rise up, it couldn't go
on forever, and it would be the Revolt of the Masses, a
true revolt of the masses, which is always pure anarchism." And Annie was thinking again it was her father's
pals talking all night when she was growing up a long
time ago in New York, while Julian plunged on, intent
on his own past. "But, anyway, one year when I came
back from a long trip abroad, my old political science
professor was gone and nobody could say or would say
where. He had simply disappeared! It shocked me. I was
still in my early twenties. But his tracts still existed, if
only in our minds, his ideas had been planted. The mind
is its own place, the best hiding place of all, and no one

can find what's hidden there, I learned that early. His was a great mind, to me at least, back then, and that single event—his disappearance—radicalized me more than anything. Yes, and during the rest of that period, those early years in Lisbon, I was really obsessed with our work. I felt—we felt we had really sacred work to do—the overthrow of our fascist dictatorship and all authoritarian regimes and all governments of any kind that took freedom from anyone!" Yes, thought Annie, as her mind wandered from his voice, out somewhere in the green fields of summer, somewhere beyond all this old rhetoric, a plain of birds somewhere, a lush plain, a meadow radiant with light. And she was watching his hands as he gestured, she wanted his hands to do more than gesture, for words and gestures were cheap on the stock exchanges of the world, especially in France with its "language of diplomacy," which was so well designed to disguise one's real thoughts in subtle nuances, so useful to both diplomats and lovers. As a hard-eyed dreamer or romantic realist (which she always considered herself to be) she wondered just how far beyond all this talking he would ever actually go. She was still a dreamer, and it seemed to her that words somehow were in the way between them, almost as if all this talking, rather than bringing them closer, kept them apart. Oh, she thought, what the brain does to the heart! She preferred his hands to be caressing her, rather than just gesturing with words, and finally he did fall silent and put his arm about her, and stroked her hair. In the diamond light and timeless air of that Paris spring, there was a headiness, a kind of sensual urgency in the soft air, and a soft breeze blew in, stirring the drapes a very little. It was one of those moments when time, as if weary of its eternal ticking, suddenly stood still, held its breath, as if someone had reached out a hand and stopped a pendulum. She closed her eyes and let herself drift, in his hands, as if they were in a drifting boat somewhere. The wild currents would catch them soon enough and carry them away, no doubt, back into the real world, Paris 1968, where everything was about to happen.

■ 4 □

Life was still a real dream, and there was a god at the beginning, if not at the end, of all joy. She felt it with him. They didn't speak of "love." To name it was to spoil it. He looked at her and thought her beautiful beyond description, even if it was all illusion. It was the look in her eyes that did it. He looked away. It was too much. He called her Anna when they made love, as if Anna were her true name and Annie a disguise. There was a kind of innocence in his nighttime voice. Down below in the street the air sounded with cries, that early April, while up under the eaves the dark doves cooed at night. Over her bed was a Rousseau painting entitled *The Lion Having Hunger* . . . , which showed a lion devouring an antelope while a panther awaited his turn to eat, and in the same room she had

Rousseau's painting called *War,* upon which the painter had written, "War passes by, *effrayante,* leaving behind it everywhere despair, tears, and ruin . . . ," while in the same room also hung *The Sleeping Gypsy* with its description by Rousseau about the wandering gypsy playing her mandoline falling into a deep sleep and "a lion, passing by chance, sniffs her but does not devour her. . . ." Down in the streets a little revolution was giving birth to much hope and euphoria, not just in France but around the world, in the U.S., in Germany and Italy and Mexico City, in Prague, in Portugal, everywhere there was a stirring, more than a stirring, a new spirit, a seething spirit. What had started as a little protest by a few angry students, by a few *enragés* at Nanterre, would spread to the Sorbonne and the Beaux-Arts and on to other schools and universities all over France, jumping then like a brush fire from students to workers everywhere. It was not just the antiquated school system which came under attack but the whole status quo of bourgeois life and its government, the whole bourgeois state questioned everywhere. The bourgeois mentality itself was the real enemy, not to mention the police mentality that ruled so many parts of the world, and her students walked out of the ateliers, and she walked out with them, for had she not been teaching that very freedom in paint which now they were acting out? And they were joining with anarchists and Trotskyites and Marxists in their condemnation of the Beaux-Arts and the Sorbonne and of the whole school system as institutions designed to keep the populace in its place in the state, designed to educate all youth to fit into the status quo of Haves and Have Nots, to become obedient *fonctionnaires.* It all would lead to a real paralysis of daily life in France, with a general strike of all the workers in France, with General de Gaulle's government in hidden confusion. There. was hope that all life could be reconceived and transformed. All the old conceptions of love, of marriage, of work, of men and women together, of the ways of looking at reality itself might never be the same again. And it all seemed possible in the spring of that year when Julian and Annie were in the heat of their love and reason.

▪ 5 ▫

In that curious dream they were living through, they were both close together and far apart, or so she thought as she looked at him close up and still saw him with her painter's eye as from a great distance. For what he professed still hardly matched up with his daily life, with his banker's life, although he said he was engaged in "certain other activities" outside the bank which he could not disclose to her, which he said were very much involved in what was going on now. They lived in a kind of a vacuum, their relationship in a still place, an isolated place into which no one else entered, since he did not introduce her to anyone in his world and he knew no one in hers. They needed no other people, completely wrapped up in themselves, and she still wanted to know more about him and where he was really coming from. In old-fashioned terms, in the terms her father used, they truly came from different classes—he from "impoverished nobility" and Annie from a working-class family in Yonkers, where her father had been a union leader, he himself the son of radical immigrants. Around this time she even had a curious dream in which she was the silent daughter in Vercors' book of the German occupation of France, *The Silence of the Sea,* in which the daughter falls in love with the cultivated Nazi officer who is billeted with her family in the provinces, and at every meal the charming officer talks about all his urbane interests and opera and art and culture, and the family always remains silent at the dinner table, the daughter too never speaks, and in Annie's dream now the German officer was transformed into Julian. Still she loved him, and she made love to him in the dream. Then one Sunday Julian suggested they go on a little excursion to the coast for the day, to Deauville, promising that he would bring "a couple of good friends" along, so she agreed, having no idea what they would be like, and the sun glinted on the station platform at Gare Saint-Lazare, where she was to meet him and his friends that day. Then she saw him, being led along the platform by two large red setters straining at their leashes, and these were his two friends of course, two friends who put their paws up to meet her but couldn't speak to tell her anything about Julian that she didn't know already. She knew very little, she knew his mind and body as in a void, in an isolated place where the two of them existed beyond the world they lived in. It was all an illusion, she thought, what they knew of each other was an illusion. Julian opened a first-class carriage door and the dogs jumped in and smelled everything and leaped around and barked as the train started up, and they had the compartment to themselves, while the dogs kept jumping up and trying to kiss her face and kept presenting their paws, first one then the other, the way dogs do, Julian laughing and saying they were still puppies but had already learned that most important single act that all French children learn, which was to shake hands, a thousand times a day. Now the train slid out of the impressionist Gare Saint-Lazare and gathered speed out into the impressionist landscape, the sun glinting on the slate roofs and on the still flowing spring waters of the Seine, and Julian said these were "true anarchist dogs," refusing to lie down and be still and conform to the bourgeois situation of the world. Their names were Noir and Rouge. Although they were both red, he said he'd named them not after Stendhal's *Rouge et Noir* but after an anarchist magazine that students had started publishing this year, black and red, the anarchist colors, and the train still picking up speed heading north and west, gliding out into the soft Norman countryside. You could see black crows in the still wet morning fields, and the bright sun broke through again, shimmering on puddles and ditches, with black-and-white cows in new green fields, a horse at a crossing, boys on cycles waving at the train. Now Julian's dogs settled down on the floor, their heads on their paws, as the train rocked onward, the sun like a thin dime flickering over the fields and the country houses with their slate roofs, and Julian was saying, "Annie, try to understand how it is with me. I have a feeling you still don't believe me at all—about my politics, I mean! You probably think I'm a real 'phony,' as they say in America, with my talk about anarchism and so forth, while all the while I'm working in the Banque de France and have an elegant apartment near Etoile, et cetera, a real phony like the Comte de Clappique in Malraux's book or something like that. But, listen, I've *always* been with the working class, even though I wasn't born into it! From my very first days in Lisbon at school, from the very first political awakening, I worked with very poor students, and worked with them against fascism, which grew, as I told you, into total opposition to *any* state. Yes, in those days, Annie, I was full of fire and impatience! I wanted a new world at once, we wanted a new world, a new life for all of us, and I threw myself into the fight, into the underground resistance. I was twenty or twenty-one, still wet behind the gills, but I saw very clearly it wasn't just the government that had us where they wanted us, they had the people where they wanted them, where they'd always been, at the bottom of the pile. It was the whole system of property and land ownership. I think I read Henry George's *Progress and Poverty* about then, which some American I met in Paris lent me, but I came to different conclusions than he did, for if it wasn't the fascists on top of the people, if it wasn't one dictator or another, it would be some other kind of gang, another bunch running the tribe for their own profit, calling themselves democrats or liberals or whatever, but it would all end up the same in the end, and the ones who seized the real power would wield it over the rest, the ones who had helped them seize it, and *they* still would have nothing much, relatively nothing, although a few sops would be thrown to them, a few bones to keep them from gnawing off your feet!" Julian looked down at his elegant shoes and his elegant dogs. "So what is an anarchist anyway, what *is* anarchism, in the end? It's the revolt inside of everybody against all that I've been describing! It's the natural revolt against *social* inequalities, not natural inequalities, which we're all born with. . . . And now the train was rolling through Evreux, halfway to the coast, and it slowed and changed its rhythms, so that the dogs awakened and jumped up, putting their paws on the windowsills, but then the train picked up speed again without stopping at the station and rocked on through back streets of that town, and Annie put her feet up as Julian went on: "And so what does our anarchist see in the world when he wakes up and looks around, when he really wakes up? He sees millions of animals and men and women, all born unequal in every way, their natural talents all unequal, no matter what kind of family they were born into, and he sees still more inequality heaped on them by all the social conventions, their original inequalities magnified by the rules of society, et cetera. And only by perseverance or plain luck can the man born poor escape from that deadlock. The dog must remain a dog, it's true, and we cannot do much about the natural inequalities, the injustices of nature. But the injustices of our social conventions, why don't we prevent them or abolish them completely? That part is within man's power. And woman's power, perhaps more so than men! The power really to stop war and violence, for instance. Remember Lysistrata! Why shouldn't all women band together and refuse to sleep with their men whenever they take to violence, whenever they start war? Soon enough, if the women stuck to it, would the swords be turned into ploughshares!" "Or shares of stock, maybe," Annie threw in, "and then you bankers could still make a little commission on the deal?" "No doubt!" Julian assented. "The banker's prerogative, to be in on everything! Even revolutions, even revolutions can be a banker's friend, if he plays it right. . . ." He fell silent. Now the train was coasting into the outskirts of another town and on through it without stopping and out again into the flatter open country, where the sea shone on the far horizon, the glittering sea coming closer. Far out now some tankers cut out dark silhouettes on the light horizon. Closer in there were fishers with sails leaning into the wind. And the wind blew inland, swaying the tops of the trees by the roadbed where loose leaves scattered. Soon they were sliding into Deauville itself, soon they were on the station platform, and through the Swiss-looking station, and along the quays of the town to the beach. The big casino was still closed, as were most of the splendid hotels, or so it seemed, and Julian took a small *cabaña* on the deserted beach, and the two of them sat back in the canvas beach chairs as the dogs bounded about and rolled on their backs in the sand, liberated. After a while Annie got up and ran along the beach and ran into the waves with the dogs while Julian watched. She came back with a handful of colored shells, brilliant with the wet salt upon them, and held them out to Julian, who took a few in his hand. Drying, the shells even now were losing their brilliance, like watercolors, never as bright when they dry. "The ceramics of the sea," said Julian, and Annie lay down with her head propped up. It was high tide and you could hear the waves lapping very slowly, washing the long strand, the sea licking its lips with its many tongues. A feeling of absolute harmony flooded over her, in waves, a groundswell of inexplicable feeling, as if there were any harmony in their lives. There was harmony in their bodies, between their bodies, Annie was thinking, but not in their so different lives, their so different ways. The voices of the world were drowned out here, in the roar of the universe inside a seashell, the strident voices of a million generations hushed in the hubbub, in the echoing void of ocean, endless in time. Yes, the sea, always there waiting, though we never think of it in our cities, even though it may lap at the edge of them, but something about it in our blood still brings us a hidden happiness in the sight and sound of it, in the memory of being still immersed in it, as in a womb we can never again recapture. Floating. Far off, the seabirds cawed and called and cried, high over. The lapping of the sea dragged all things into dream. Julian lay back, his eyes closed, in his canvas chair. He was like a hawk, a seabird, a bird of prey, an osprey who makes its nest at sea. He must have had ancestors who went to sea, in Portuguese men-of-war. The scar on his cheek a tiny sea urchin.

■ 6 □

Back in Paris late that night, or early morning, back in her bed, feeling small and intense, she dreamt of the sea, and the sea seemed to sing, half in French, half in English. Julian in her dream was in the sea, swimming, far out, they were both in the warm sea, it was not winter, the sea was a crystal and they revolved in it, their bodies floating upon each other, with *une attirance réciproque, une attirance atroce,* a terrible attraction for each other, like magnets even the sea could not keep apart, could not pull apart. She heard Julian's voice as in an awkward translation, echoing in a seashell, and his voice laughed, "How lovely *uncivilization* is!" and they were naked in the sea, some phallic god controlling them, twisting them about toward some core of light on the surface of the sea. They floated up to it, up into it, toward that core of flashing light, whirling light, as inside some ancient movie camera or stereopticon upon which flashed multiple obscene images of copulation, with Latin titles as on bronze plaques fished up from the Baths of Nero, and the sea sang the names of those images, *Venere Aversa, More Canino, Flexio Gallinacea, Saltus Subversum, Inverso Paligrada,* a perverted litany sounding with sea gongs undersea, over and over, echoing. Somewhere a priapic god laughed derisive in a cave, and she awoke in the dark dawn and raised her head and looked out over the rooftops of Paris, while a dove up under the eaves moaned its mantra, a long way from the sea where she could no longer grasp the body of Julian, and the priapic god floated up, leering in her face and singing to her a tragic song about mixing love with reason, "Oh, they are oil and water," sang the god in her sleep, and Julian's body sank away in the flood of it, as other swimmers with erect phalluses floated obscenely toward her.

■ 7 □

"**O**h, I am not the Comte de Clappique!" Julian was laughing as they sat out on the tiny terrace of the Café des Artistes on the Place Contrescarpe in her neighborhood. "But neither am I Monsieur Ferral!" For the Comte de Clappique in Malraux's *Man's Fate* was probably a double agent, betraying both sides in the Chinese revolution whenever necessary to save his skin, whereas Monsieur Ferral was the banker president of the French Chamber of Commerce in Shanghai. Julian despite his joking was still intent upon persuading Annie that he was indeed on the right side, on the side of her students in the present situation, which was developing from a revolt into a real revolution, even though life on a sunny afternoon might seem to be going on as it had forever and ever, even as now under the plane trees out in the little square a group of poor young musicians had set up and started to play slow old waltzes, with a bent tuba, an accordion, a sax, and an old drum, sounding forth their nostalgia into the Sunday air, echoing up the side streets. Now half a dozen small children came out of doorways and stood right in front of the musicians, and one small dog on a yellow leash tied to an ornate iron lamppost started barking, as an old crone with shawl and cane stopped and turned around to listen, while winos laid out in the sun on the cobbles of the square raised their rummy heads. Now a very old couple with empty shopping bags on their way across the square stopped and very, very slowly started dancing together, without putting down the bags, not touching, the old man courtly, turning about the feeble old lady, who held herself very straight, barely moving her feet, he shorter than she, wearing a white golf cap and old white linen suit and sandals, with dark glasses as if perhaps he were half blind, and she with white shoulder-length hair, white skirt and lace blouse, with short red gym socks and open-toed sandals, and the accordion's sad yearning voice took over, like the voice of the past itself, and the couple danced on so slowly, hardly moving, as if time too had slowed down and would last forever, as if the old couple might still live forever, just as they were there, dancing on. Annie wondered if she would *ever* have a relationship like that, as she imagined the old couple's, a relationship that would go on and on, through decades, for the rest of life. She thought back to another spring when she had fallen in love with one of her teachers at the Art Students League, he one of the great teachers, a man in his sixties then, what the students called "an old rad," of the thirties generation, one of the WPA artists who went around with the old

Partisan Review crowd, but at this time, her time, he was not very far away from retirement and used to like to have some of his favorite students come up to his flat on West End Avenue on Sundays and drink beer and talk about painting and politics. There didn't seem to be any woman in residence at his house, and it was only much later she found out the truth, but then that summer back then after classes were over for the year she used to drop in now and then and usually found him alone in his huge studio and always glad to see her. Looking back now she could see that she was the one who had made the advances, although he certainly did respond with affection. But in the end it came out, it all came out that he was very gay, and there was no way around it. A very solitary man, living by himself and still living for his students, and Annie didn't stop seeing him, but in the end she had to leave, she had to move on, with her own needs, and he gave her a silver ring set with a scarab which she still had and still wore. In addition to that he gave her much more, he showed her the artist as perpetual enemy of the state, as gadfly of the state, the artist as the total enemy of all the organized forces that bore down on the free individual everywhere, the artist as the bearer of Eros, as bearer of the life force itself, as bearer of love, in a world seemingly bent on destroying all that, Eros versus civilization, life against death. Yes, in his printmaking classes you learned not only stone lithography and drypoint etching, you also learned you had to use that art to say something important, not just a bunch of minimalist nothingness. You learned the radical tradition of the WPA artists and muralists. "Speak up and stop mumbling!" he would yell at them when he bent over their work and saw that the drawing was saying nothing. And it was strange, she reflected now, how his ideas were like Julian's, as now Julian had fallen silent, watching the musicians in the square, but suddenly then in the middle of that sunny idyll came a dissident sound from down the Rue Mouffetard, the sound of drums beaten by students carrying placards who now came streaming into the Place Contrescarpe, circling the still-playing musicians and the old couple, who now stopped dancing and hurried off down the street. And the three students with drums led a straggling line around the little square, with more of them pouring in all the time, waving placards and banners upon which were scrawled and painted the first murmurings of that wild new spirit of rebellion. Among them were posters she recognized as having been done by the poster brigades at the Beaux-Arts, some by her students, some of them indeed in the style of WPA artists but with messages hardly dreamed of in the American thirties:

Alcohol kills: Take LSD

THE YOUNG MAKE LOVE, THE OLD MAKE OBSCENE GESTURES

I'M A GROUCHO MARXIST

"Revolution is the ecstasy of history"

MAKE LOVE AND BEGIN AGAIN

POWER TO THE IMAGINATION!

"Nous sommes tous les enragés"—Ortega y Gasset

TO FORBID IS FORBIDDEN

Open the Windows of Your Heart

MAKE LOVE NOT WAR

THE SORBONNE IS THE STALINGRAD OF THE REVOLUTION!

■ 8 □

Annie and Julian too were swept along, if not swept away, by the parading students, and they found themselves carried along in the crowd as it struggled out of the Place Contrescarpe and downhill to the Ecole Polytechnique, where they poured into the courtyard and gardens of the school and filled them, parading around and around the main court, while some Polytech students who were *not* with them hooted and heckled from upstairs windows and emptied scrapbaskets and pails of water on them, putting up their own handwritten signs like FRENCH FOR THE FRENCH and GO HOME TO PAPA, and then just before dark the police came careening up the steep streets in their paddy wagons with their sirens screaming as the students immediately began to disperse, running up all the side streets and into any open stores or restaurants or cafés or apartment buildings in the neighborhood, so that by the time the gendarmes piled out of their wagons into the courtyard of the Polytechnique there was little left for them to do except pick up the trash, which they scorned to do. Julian and Annie had run down the Rue Descartes to her building and then up the winding five flights of stairs, throwing open the doors on her balcony to check the action below. Suddenly a calm had descended, and it was almost as if nothing had happened at all, as if it were just another normal night in Paris with everyone behind their closed doors living their private bourgeois lives. Annie and Julian poured themselves drinks and sat down. Julian said: "It's a long time since my student days, yet it still hasn't happened, the real 'revolution' hasn't happened yet, it's the same old story, the students divided against themselves as before, and the anarchists and the Marxists still on the same side but still violently opposed to each other, the students and the workers together but not together, each still unable to really understand the other, still with wildly different goals, even though come together against the state. . . ." "So what else is new?" said Annie, laughing, hoping to head off another discourse. But Julian was obsessed as usual and pressed on: "Just like in Lisbon . . . but . . . let me go back to the very beginning! When I first saw the light of Lisbon we were living in a huge old flat which my father had managed somehow to hold on to in the general *chute* of our fortunes. It was at the top of an old, old building which looked like it was always about to fall down—at 56 Antonio Augusta Aguiar. I loved all the cats that lived on the tile roofs. . . . But anyway my old father died of consumption—and my mother was living by selling family silver and furniture, and I remember how bare the apartment was. The light shone on the old polished wood floor in our living room where I lay on a blanket with my toys. I remember how I reached out and tried to grasp the light and how it passed on to my hand yet still I could not grasp it, and the first word I ever said, according to my mother, was *luz*. I remember also that I was usually hungry, in that big elegant flat, in the best part of town. My mother had to give up nursing me too early, I think, and I seemed to have a constant hunger and a constant thirst that water did not assuage. I couldn't have been more than a year old and I remember vividly the sunlight on the polished floor, shining, like gold, like a shadow of gold on the old wood, and my mother leaning over, I could see the dark inside of her mouth with a gold filling as she laughed over me where I lay, her perfume, a light perfume, enveloped me in the sunlight. There were birds on the window ledge, turning about in the sunlight, casting their purple shadows into the room, their long thin shadows, upon the oak floor, and then they all flew off at once, with small cries, and my mother straightened up and went out, probably only into the next room, but it could have been around the world and forever, for all I knew. There was only her presence or her absence in my life, she was there or not there, and it was forever before she came back. Hunger and thirst, hunger and love! Yes, that was it. . . . I remember when she first didn't come back. I must have been three by then. One day she simply didn't come back, she simply wasn't there any longer. And then it was later and my aunt in France taking care of me. I went to school there for a while, down near the Spanish border in France, and another aunt came and took me back to Portugal, to Castelo Branco, that mountain town, way up near the Spanish border on that side, and I went to the local school run by the nuns. We had enough to eat but I always had that feeling of hunger and thirst, as if something were missing. I didn't know what it was I missed, perhaps it was 'light' because I remember the dark clouds always over the mountains, which seemed to shed their shadows directly on us. The water from the mountains that ran in the gutters was dark, it bore no sunlight, and in the summer the rains beat down, and the wind blew the sun away with its fine dust. I must have been ten by then. . . ." Julian paused, ran a hand through his hair, got up and looked out at the sky, and then turned back to Annie and went on: "Whatever it was I wanted—it was something intangible which I was incapable of grasping, unable to articulate anything at that dumb age—at thirteen or fourteen. I felt as if I knew nothing about anything—about anything important—about what made life go round. The nuns didn't teach it. They seemed to teach the opposite, to hide the true facts of life from us. They taught us what they wanted us to see, and it seemed to me a world of darkness. Their god is what they wanted us to see, nothing else, we little devils, fierce little barbarians full of fierce feelings and hungers, snot-nosed little rebels looking for a way out of that darkness. The god they were always praying to was a dark god, a vengeful god, the god of the Spanish. Even though the Portuguese always turned their back on Spain (and French their second language, not Spanish) in Portugal everything bad still seemed to come from Spain, including fascism! Bad wine and bad marriages came from Spain! Like Spain, the Portuguese churches were full of black Christs, writhing on their black crosses, dripping tears of black blood. We had to go to catechism in the vaults of one of these churches, and the nuns came down the dark Gothic passageways of those vaults, their black capes flapping like huge desolate wings, like angels of death they flew toward us. I turned and ran out, only to be dragged back, by those kind but iron hands, more like claws. . . . It seemed they were bent on keeping us from the light. They taught us darkness and death, the eternal wringing of hands and desolate prayers to Someone we could never see, who was always shrouded in darkness, some disembodied being who simply wasn't there, or anywhere. I prayed to my dead mother instead, or my dead father—mostly it was her. It seemed the nuns and in fact everyone in the grown-up world was engaged in a huge conspiracy to keep us from the light and from any real knowledge of the world. What really made life go, what really made men and women and animals go was never mentioned, was, it seemed, carefully hidden away from us. Everything they gave us to read was part of this great conspiracy, and I read everything I could find. I devoured the town library, such as it was, and once in a while I came upon a magazine that gave me some inkling of the outside world, of real life. It was much later on, when I was at the university in Lisbon, that I realized it was not just the nuns and the people of that ignorant mountain town who were engaged in this conspiracy to keep us ignorant—it was the whole society that was doing it, everyone was engaged in doing it—a kind of mass self-deception the whole populace was engaged in, without even realizing it, certainly encouraged by vested interests everywhere—a deception which not only religion but all the mores of society continually reinforced—denying first off that we were animals with animal instincts, et cetera. What had become of *nature?* We were to act as if nature no longer existed in us, inside ourselves, as if we all didn't have the same animal urges. And there was only one acceptable way for us to act, to acquiesce in the huge conspiracy. Now it seems a cliché to say it like that, but back then, back then I was barely able to see it, to intuit even a hazy idea of it. . . ." Julian paused again and sipped his drink, and Annie got up and stood in the doorway to the balcony, looking up at the night sky. The night was warm, and there was something in the air that excited her, a sensual joy, in the deceptively still evening, a *douceur* that she had only known in Paris, under the grey roofs or out in the gardens like Luxembourg, where even the stone statues seemed to have a sensual softness. There was no other city she knew that had this strange erotic quality in its gardens and its streets, in the very air itself, a sensual mystery that enveloped everything. She felt the euphoria that comes with love or lust, as he came up behind her now and put his arms around her and held her. "You were saying?" she said. The same euphoria, it seemed, did not exactly grip him, as he went on: "I used to wonder if my dog felt the same as I did, with the same urges. Under a microscope, when I got to the university, I found protozoa had them too—the same urge to life, the same urge to 'gestate,' to reproduce. So that's what love came down to, I thought. That's all it is, I thought, having never yet fallen in love! I was sixteen by then, with a body full of crazy hungers and no way to satisfy them. There was a gang of us, all bursting at the seams, fresh from the convent school, suddenly loose in Lisbon, at the university. Bursting at the seams, indeed! A comical situation, if we could have seen ourselves. . . . Lisbon, a decadent city, a small Rome, also built on little hills, a teeming little hive, full of us animals. . . ." "And then?" asked Annie. "And then I met a woman named Annie." "Haven't you skipped a few years and a few women?" "Just as well," he answered, with a small laugh. "You don't want me to be here all night, do you?"

■ 9 □

When Annie didn't answer, he sat her down on the couch and put his arms around her and kissed her. She broke away from him and lay by herself, looking away, and he put his arms around her again. Somewhere in the building someone was playing an old Django Reinhardt record, and the sound of his guitar echoed faintly, until they fell asleep like that, upon the couch. In her sleep she held him very close, there was an illusion of oneness between them, almost a feeling of "I am you," except reason raised its old bald head, so that in her fitful dream she saw old man reason coming toward her looking absurdly like Jean-Paul Sartre, looking steadily at her through his very thick glasses, a half-smoked Gaulois between his lips, the smoke in his eyes, and Annie in her dream absurdly became a young Simone de Beauvoir, and Sartre was saying to her over and over, "Engagés! Enragés! Engagés!" But the wind blew them away, and reason came at her again looking like a Borgia carrying a chastity belt from La Musée de Guerre, and somewhere a priapic god laughed and leered again, in the depths of her dream, raising its phallic head. Sometime then a real wind came up and a heavy rain started falling, lashing the windowpanes, coming in the open doors, fingers of rain in the dark room. They slept on, and the sky cleared, and she dreamt on, in that lost time before dawn which is neither night nor morning, and he stirred and came over her, a soft sound in his throat, a different voice from his waking voice, much softer, yet a masculine sound, like an animal, an intelligent beast, a dreaming animal, and they like dreaming animals made love in the first light, in which mirrors reflecting their selves floated up, and the two mirrors merged into one mirror, their two images merged into one image reflected in a sea of other bodies, hordes of bodies merging into a horizon made of flesh and lost in the tide of morning, in a sleep of unchained prisoners, escapees who had been chained to rocks of reason upon steep mountains lost undersea, and they swam upward toward the light, the light of their lives that had always been hidden over the horizon, or hidden above the surface of the water which they could not see through, as one could not see the risen shore from undersea, could not see the far islands or figures close up. Close up now, his face came over hers, and she saw his face as if for the first time, a face from which some masks seemed to have fallen, one after another, as an onion sheds its rings, down and down to the heart of it, to the heart of—of nothing—of nothing! Was there to be finally nothing there, nothing at the heart of him, of it, of "love," or whatever one wanted to call it, nothing in the end at the heart of life itself, only a skin wearing down to the very zero heart of existence? Face-to-face in her dream with the inner nothingness of existence, and the mind a *camera obscura* in which all revolved in shadows cast upon the inner walls, in the bent mirrors of her dream, turning and returning through the sea, a house of mirrors drifting round her in which was reflected nothing but themselves, *la vida un sueño real.* His body stirred and floated away, borne away by foreign currents, by alien gulf streams it seemed impossible to swim against, his body broke the surface and disappeared into the very heart of light, while she sank back and back, through the deep swirling waters, into the deep pearl, the final mystery. . . . When she awoke, he was gone. He'd left a note on the table: "I love you like myself." In English. She could hear his accent, the gruff gentleness in his voice, his other voice. "Like myself. . . ." It was the dream again, the double mirrors. Narcissus and friend. Priapus over the stone pool. One on one. In waves and waves of lust, or was it love, over and over. "If you tell me love is all an illusion—if you tell me all is illusion," he had said once, "then it is."

▪ 10 ◻

It was still April, that fertile month which isn't the cruelest in Paris, and they walked by the Seine another sunny Sunday morning, just another pair of Paris lovers, down along the quays where the ochre water coursed, the river swollen with spring rains. But they weren't just another pair of lovers, they were so uniquely themselves, aware of the uniqueness of each other, in the first awakened state of that love, strangely happy in each other, in having "found" each other, through the mazes, each so alive in the new experience of the other. It had grown on them, each not fully aware of what was happening, and now it engulfed them. Up to a point. It was an April that had happened to many and only to them, it could only have happened in Paris and could have happened anywhere else, it was

Paris in the spring and it could have been anywhere anytime where they were together. Neither would believe in it, yet they did. "Ils flânaient sur le Pont des Arts, du côté de l'Ile Saint-Louis, dès premières heures du matin. . . ." Some years later she came upon this passage in a memoir by a French lover of poet Keith Barnes, and she saw herself and Julian in it, walking the night streets and the early morning streets of Paris, along the quiet quays in the early morning, the light growing. There was no English word for *flânaient.* "Strolled" wouldn't do. They wandered the streets, for hours without destination, the sidewalks stretching out before them like so many paths of light still to be explored, everything alive with their own pulse, the birds on rooftops, owls in eaves at night, by dark grottoes of Saint-Julien-le-Pauvre. It was a somehow unreal dream from which they returned in the daytime, separated, in their own daytime lives, and what was happening in those daytime streets brought them always back to reality. It was a cruel spring in many ways, for youth in the streets. "We are all *enragés,"* Julian was saying one of those days, in his obsessed way. "All of us, all us animals on earth, not just Daniel Cohn-Bendit and a handful of students at Nanterre and the 'Movement of March Twenty-second'—we're all of course 'enraged' by the fact we all have to die sometime, sooner or later. 'Rage, rage against the dying of the light,' the poet said. When I was one week old I reached for the light in a window, for the sun, and when I was eighteen I didn't know what I wanted but I had more than my share of that strange 'rage to live.' My old aunt died that year, when I was eighteen, and in the summer that year, at the end of my first year at the university, I went off to Paris on my own. There were relatives, still, in the south of France, but I wanted to be on my own. Here, in Paris, it was one of those eternal moments, the moment when you sense yourself out in the world really on your own for the first time—even if penniless, which I almost was. But free! In Paris, then, 'je rôdais, je flânais, je planais,' as Blaise Cendrars said—I roamed, I wandered, I floated. Yes, Cendrars was my poet-hero then—he who had written 'En ce temps-là, j'étais dans mon adolescence . . . et mon adolescence était alors si ardente et si folle. . . . Et tous les jours et toutes les femmes dans les cafés' . . . It isn't as good as in English: 'And all the days and all the women in cafés and all the glasses, I would have liked to drink them all and break them. . . . And all the windows and all the lives, and all the wheels of carriages turning and turning on the—on the *mauvais pavés*. And I wanted to plunge them all in a furnace of swords . . . all the strange bodies naked under their clothes, all the bodies that drove me crazy—' " Julian was fairly carried away, quoting Cendrars, and he stopped short, and they both laughed and sat down on a bench on the quay right behind Notre-Dame, with its huge buttresses rising up in front of them. "Well, there it is," Julian resumed, gesturing, "the whole monstrous monument to medieval superstition! An insult to human reason, with its germ-ridden holy-water stoups! Dip your hand in that never-washed trough and smear it on your forehead—a potent solution, indeed. Dip your hand in and die. Bow down! An odor of rotten eggs, as from a dead hen! And I'm back with those angels of death at Castelo Branco, still trying to escape them and their big guilty Original Sin they were still trying to lay on us. Bow down! for I am the Lord of Creation. You have sinned by the very act of coming on earth, by the very act of becoming flesh, and ye shall suffer for it, forever and ever, amen. Bow down! For there is Hell to pay! Dante

meeting Beatrice by the river had to shake off the shack-
les to see her, the medieval chains, to see her as pure
being, unknown to 'sin'. . . . There were some *clochards* lying around on the pavement by the water, sun-
ning themselves, and an old dame came along with her
sacks and bundles of clothes, which caused one of the
men to rise up and hoot at her, as if he were calling
pigs. "Where you been," he shouted at her, "since I seen
you last in the sack!" And the other men all raised up
and howled at her, roaring with laughter and rolling over.
"Fils de pute!" she roared back at them, fumbling in her
bags and stumbling on down the quay, as three elegant
gendarmes carrying walkie-talkies came up in their black
uniforms with sidearms and billy clubs and surrounded
the bums and went from one to the other, demanding
their papers and inspecting them, as one cop used his
radio; but suddenly the cops all shrugged their shoul-
ders and turned away up the quay, leaving the *clochards*
where they would always be and nothing to be done
about it, while Annie and Julian watched. "The goddamn
state," Julian exclaimed in English. "I wish I could grind
it down with my teeth!" Annie had never heard him use
such a fierce tone before. "The cops . . ." he went on,
"they're the same the world over, aren't they—the cop
mentality the same in every country, no matter what color
the uniform, and everywhere the cops are almost the
only visible image that people have of the state, and *are*
the state to most people, especially to the poor, for behind every little gendarme in his de Gaulle hat there are
a hundred thousand like him around the world, holding
the system together, the 'Patronat,' the big employers,
and behind them all the armies of the world—press a
button, if a bum answers back too rudely, and—wham,
off you go—the whole bloody establishment falls on

him—Disraeli's two nations. . . ." "Right on, professor," said Annie lightly as they got up and turned to climb the long stone stairs up to the street. It was always like rejoining the live reality of the world when you went back up to the street from the quays, as at Place Saint-Michel, where now there was graffiti everywhere on the walls and on the sidewalks, and it was the students speaking in chalk and spray paint:

"FRENCH FOR THE FRENCH" = FASCIST SLOGAN

DEATH TO THE STATE

"In revolution there are two kinds of people:
Those who make it and those who profit from it."
—Napoleon

"The tears of the philistines
Are the nectar of the gods"

U.S. DEFEAT THE MARINES

UNDER THE PAVING STONES IS THE BEACH!

THE BARRICADE CLOSING THE STREET OPENS THE WAY

ROME BERLIN MADRID PRAGUE VARSOVIE PARIS THE WORLD!

Open the Doors of Asylums Prisons and
Other "Faculties"

I DECLARE THE STATE OF PERMANENT HAPPINESS!

"The more I make love, the more I want revolution,
The more I make revolution, the more I want to
make love"

POETRY IN THE STREET!

Rêve + Evolution = Revolution

You need RED to get out of darkness

"One has to carry a chaos inside oneself
in order to bring into the world
a dancing star"

A COP SLEEPS IN EACH OF US: YOU HAVE TO KILL HIM
——CULTURAL AGITATION COMMITTEE

EMBRACE YOUR LOVER
WITHOUT DROPPING YOUR GUN

While on the sidewalk of the Pont Neuf a little farther along, Annie and Julian came upon a yellow chalk portrait of the folk singer Leo Ferré, which a street artist had left, with a verse scrawled next to it, and an appeal for spare change:

A drawing on the sidewalk
to make you change your pace
On the path of love and hope
to save the race!
MERCI (1 F ou 2 F s.v.p.)

And Annie sat down on a curb of the bridge and took out her sketchbook and began to draw an idea for a poster, when all of a sudden out of a side street across the Place Saint-Michel came a wailing wild ragged band of American poets singing and shouting that the Poetry Police were coming to save them, the Poetry Police were coming to save them all from death, Captain Poetry was coming to save the world from itself, to make the world safe for beauty and love, the Poetry Police had arrived to clean up the mass mess, the Poetry Police were about to descend in parachutes made from the pages of obscene dictionaries, the Poetry Police were about to land simultaneously in the central squares of forty-two major cities, having chartered all the planes in the world and being furnished with free seats for an endless passage since all were *poids net,* the Poetry Police were about to land simultaneously on the tops of the tallest buildings and bridges and monuments and fortifications of the world and take complete command of the rapidly deteriorating world situation, the Poetry Police were about to invade Geneva and decide once and for all what the shape of the table should be at all future peace conferences, the Poetry Police were about to consolidate their positions simultaneously in all parts of the world by climbing onto the backs and hanging onto the necks of everyone and shouting true profound wiggy formulas for eternal mad salvation, the Poetry Police were about to capture all libraries, newspapers, printing presses, and automats, and force their proprietors at pen's point to print nothing henceforth but headlines of pure poetry and menus of pure love, every day's papers to be filled with nothing henceforth but pure poetry stories giving the latest positions and poses and appearances and manifestations and demonstrations of pure beauty made out of the whole cloth of naked reality itself as well as the latest reports on the latest actions of love throughout the universe, publishing all the love that was fit to print and all the love that was fit to kill, but refusing to publish any stories or headlines or pictures on any other subject at all since no other subject was News anymore, and even the great unretouchable editors of *Death Magazine* in their high glass offices would raise their venetian blinders, and student painters from the Beaux-Arts wrote great blazing paintings on second-story walls running the length of every street, while poets wrote great blazing poems on the unwinding toilet paper, and these great endless mad poems were draped across the streets and boulevards, from streetlamp to streetlamp, and dropped in swirls around the heads of elderly civilians who gobbled them up, fought over them, and rushed home to paste them up on shaving mirrors and on union barber poles and on the walls of union warehouses and on the backsides of the Chamber of Deputies, the Conciergerie, the Opéra and the Opéra Comique and the Cirque Medrano, where circling circus horses and their standing bareback riders read them and fell down rapt but singing in the sawdust, as well as on the front walls of every American Express and every suburban apartment building in the outskirts of all cities and on the side doors of all churches and temples, with the world *love* underlined wherever it occurred in a poem, and the Poetry Revolution was growing, the Poetry Revolution was shaking, transforming existence and civilization as it rolled down around the corner of the Boule Miche and down the Boulevard Saint-Germain toward Odéon, where Danton watched over a Métro entrance and pocket watches hung from trees each with a different time swinging in the breeze but all of them indicating it was later than you think, while crowds of black berets and herds of sandals came floating and staggering and flying out of the Café Mabillon and the Pergola to join the much-belated Poetry Revolution, while three thousand nine hundred and forty-two alumni of the Académie Duncan came streaming out of the Rue de Seine combing their hair with Grecian lyres and breathing heavily into their lovers' ears. . . .

■ || □

It was the very last of April, and there was a tension and an excitement in the air, precursor of that revolutionary euphoria that sweeps through the streets when the first decisive insurrections have succeeded, a feeling of euphoria and weightlessness, as if dead laws of everyday life keeping everyone in their places have suddenly been dissolved. It was contagious—and deceptive. For here it hadn't quite happened yet, and perhaps never would. The fruit was ripe, but it hadn't fallen. The government and most of the press were still able to call it *un frisson,* a tremor, a little disturbance, a "little student agitation," or simply a "display of emotion." Yes, *une Emotion* they called it in French, with a capital *E,* something that could be contained, that could be controlled with a little adult com-

mon sense, a little *raison*. The king would send a troop
of light cavalry, as in the seventeenth century, and all
would be contained, *contrôlé*, after a *bagarre* or two.
Meanwhile the special tac units—the CRS—the Special
Riot Police, with their truncheons and black space helmets and black shields, were formed up in alleys and
side streets all around the *quartier* of the Sorbonne,
leaning against dark walls or sitting silent in their black
marias, waiting. You could see their gas masks hung up
behind them on racks in the wagons. While at the main
intersections, at the *carrefour* of Saint-Michel and Saint-
Germain, and around the Place Saint-Michel, the so elegant gendarmes in pillbox hats and white gloves directed traffic as usual, *la gloire de France* for all to see
in the person of every stiff gendarme in the image of Le
Général himself. And there had been a rally in the Place
de la Sorbonne, and Annie was there along with some
of her students, listening to the hot speeches. The tension was building, still wasn't strong enough to burst
out, and eventually the crowd began drifting apart. It
was noon by then, and Annie, feeling at loose ends, tele-
phoned Julian from a booth on the Boule Miche, to see
if he was free for lunch. They made a rendezvous near
the Bourse, near his bank, and so then there he was,
waiting for her in the back of the elegant little restaurant, the kind that still had lace curtains on brass rods at
the windows. He had the morning papers and was reading the reports. The old-line *Figaro* didn't have much at
all, trying to ignore what was happening, especially in
Paris. In the restaurant too you would never know there
was anything violent fomenting just across town, just
across the river. "Paris doesn't like to be disturbed, does
it?" said Annie, by way of greeting. "Especially around
the Stock Exchange," said Julian, surveying the elegant

clientele of the old restaurant. An ancient waiter actually wearing a pince-nez came bowing up, took their order, and tottered off, looking like a Degas dancing master. It was a long way from the Place de la Sorbonne. The lace curtains, the brightly polished brass railings, the discrete booths with lush leather banquettes, the elderly dame in black lace at the *caisse,* gave the impression of still being deep in the nineteenth century, caught forever in an impressionist painting, and one almost expected to hear the soft clop-clop of carriage horses outside. "I should have brought a sketchbook," Annie said, as she began drawing on the menu, which seemed perhaps to embarrass Julian a very little. He fidgeted. "Well, if you can do a Daumier or a Goya . . ." he began. "Imagination au Pouvoir?" said Annie, drawing the slogan at the top of the *carte,* and Julian decided to enjoy himself, lifting his glass of wine. "Go ahead on the tablecloth too! After all, it's in the great tradition. They all did it, the impressionists did it, Picasso did it, the symbolists and dadaists and surrealists did it, they all drew on table-cloths, except they were paper tablecloths, and then of course they took the paper back to their studios and copied it on canvas sometimes, and got their whole world down on canvas, for everyone to dream about today—" "As if that world still existed," Annie put in, drawing on the menu. "Just like all these elegant people in this restaurant still think it still exists—nothing but a painter's dream forever and ever!" Julian wasn't laughing anymore, watching her draw contorted bourgeois figures in top hats and picture hats, writhing on the paper, hanging on the phrases of the *haute cuisine,* running off the elegant page, dropping off, as it were, into the real world of 1968 under the students' revolutionary slogan "Imagination au Pouvoir!" It was a cry heard around the world that year, a cry of rebellion everywhere, more than a "hippie rebellion." Annie was still drawing when the soup came, and she continued, pushing it aside. "I have this fantasy," she went on, "this painter's fantasy about Paris, which should really be called L'Huile-sur-Toile—Oil-on-Canvas, as they say in the descriptions of paintings in museums. So once upon a time there was this little village called L'Huile-sur-Toile—a little tiny village on a little tiny river called the Toile. Now, that was a very long time ago, maybe in the Middle Ages or earlier still. Before that, painters mostly painted on wood—*huile-sur-bois*—but then, L'Huile-sur-Toile started growing, and more and more painters constructed *paysages* all around the banks of the Toile, and the little town grew larger and larger and larger, with all kinds of different neighborhoods or *quartiers* springing up, all built in different styles, and the styles swept the town from one end to the other, age upon age the styles changed, like the changes in architecture itself, like the changes in dress and in life-styles. There was the pastoral and then the Gothic *quartier* and then the baroque *quartier,* and eventually the symbolist and the surrealist and every kind of neighborhood that any artist could imagine. But at first there was mostly darkness on the Toile, because it was still the Dark Ages, and they only had candles and oil lamps and no electricity, and their heads were full of shadows and superstition and darkness too. But—but gradually the light grew in the heart of darkness, at first only a faint light in the distant sky, behind the dark landscape, behind the dark buildings along the Toile, and then it broke through over the rooftops, and flooded the Toile itself. Then the forces of darkness entrenched themselves on the Right Bank and the forces of light took the Left Bank as theirs, so that from the earliest

times the reactionary Right faced the avant-garde pro-
gressive liberal Left, and each viewed the other suspi-
ciously, each considering The Other Side to be treach-
erous territory, alien land. But the light kept growing,
and then in the nineteenth century the first impressionists came marching down the boulevards from Montmartre to the river's edge, all of them looking obses-
sively for light and nothing but light, their easels under
arm. And they strolled along the Toile and set up their
easels and started painting the light, and some of them
crossed over to the Left but many remained on the Right,
where most of them had been born in good bourgeois
families. But they all were obsessed with light and many
of them didn't care where it came from or where it would
lead them, they were not concerned with the sociology
or the politics of L'Huile-sur-Toile. And their style swept
the city and the suburbs and the countryside all up and
down the Toile, as far as the eye could see in the new
light, and swept even down to the far sea, through Nor-
mandy to Honfleur and back again, back past the Grande
Jatte and the promenades and quays all along the Toile,
and in the center of Paris-sur-Toile the good burghers
of the city clapped their hands and danced and sang the
'Marseillaise' and other stirring nationalist anthems, while
the impressionists and the postimpressionists kept on
painting everything in sight, including the Opéra and
their own dear Bourse right here. And they painted Notre-
Dame over and over, although neither the Right nor the
Left could really claim the Church as being exclusively
theirs, since it stood in the middle of the river on the
Ile de la Cité, although many times the towers seemed
to tilt to the Right and at rare times to the Left. There
was one gang of artists who had descended as impressionists from their Bateau Ivre high on the Right in

Montmartre, and this gang of impressionists refused to
stick to the same style of painting with their newfound
light but insisted on constantly changing their styles. Their
leader was Picasso, who constantly broke up the old formulas and forged new styles of seeing and invented
cubism and painted everything all over in cubes and then
destroyed them, after which came the dadaists and surrealists and symbolists and other ists and the taxis of the
Marne and the First World War, while the painters all
kept repainting the landscape of the Toile over and over,
until finally the Spanish Civil War ushered in the Second
World War, and with the Second War came the American invaders, and they came, they saw, they conquered
but then didn't leave as they were supposed to, but stayed
on to take advantage of the very good exchange on the
American dollar and to take advantage of the very good
light for painting. Then these foreigners and others of
their ilk from all over the world also started repainting
the landscape of the Toile, only this time it was no longer
recognizable as the adorable little *bourg* it had always
been. It all began to look like a huge imitation abstract-
expressionist canvas by Franz Kline or Willem de Kooning, while the Bourse went on looking just like it always
had in impressionist pictures, with its inhabitants still
looking and thinking like their impressionist portraits.
And then General de Gaulle himself came in here, into
this very restaurant, and he bowed and saluted and bowed
again, without taking off his pillbox hat or even offering
to check it, all the while murmuring to himself, 'La Gloire,
oui, c'est La Gloire!' And everyone rushed into the streets
of L'Huile-sur-Toile waving the tricolor and shouting,
'Don't change anything, ever! Don't rock the boat! The
Left Bank doesn't exist!' And everyone went around acting as if the world of L'Huile-sur-Toile was perfect and

no need to change anything ever, everything should go on as it always had on the avenues of La Grande République. But, but the students, *alors, merde,* the students—*ces enragés, ces chienlits*—were hungry and bored, and they had had enough of All That, they wanted an entirely new mix of colors, an entirely new palette, entirely new tools and new types of brushes to paint with, and they used spray paint on everything. They woke up the workers everywhere, they inspired the hunger strikers, and every other brand of forgotten humanity came pouring out of the side streets—the anarchists and the Trotskyists and the communists who hated everyone else, especially the anarchists, they all began to unite, because they were all hungry and fed up with the flat flabby *ancien régime* and with de Gaulle's *grandeur,* which didn't include them. They were all totally frustrated by the plutocracy that ruled the world even beyond the Toile, and they wanted to focus a huge magnifying glass on the canvas of the whole world and concentrate the new light on the very center of that canvas until it caught fire and burned a hole right through the whole landscape!" This time it was Annie who was fairly carried away, her voice tending to rise to a higher octave, so that now the antique waiter with the raised eyebrows came hurrying up, and Annie broke off and sat back, looking at Julian, who sat silent looking at her as if he had never really seen her before. Then he raised his glass to her, smiling in her eyes, and drank, as she spooned her cold soup. Then after a while Julian signed a chit, and they went out together into the loud afternoon traffic that crept past the Bourse, the multicolored cars like myriad drops of paint flowing over an immense abstract-impressionist landscape whose perspective had long ago been destroyed.

▪ 12 ▫

She of the sloping breasts
and shy smile, she with her long auburn hair out of a
Klimt painting, she was one of those living dots of glow-
ing paint lost in a vast Jackson Pollock canvas, in the
flowing *paysage* without perspective, dissolved in that so
feminine landscape, that *paysage séduisant* which was
still Paris. But now it had taken on a harsher, more hard-
edge aspect, as Annie hurried through the hard traffic
that raped the female city every day. Annie had work to
do. Her classes weren't meeting anymore, and she out
on strike with her students; but she headed back across
the river now to the Beaux-Arts and up to the big grey
atelier at the top of the oldest of the old buildings. And
there she confronted her paintings, alone. It was a con-
frontation all painters knew and could not avoid. Sooner

or later you had to face them. Even when she stacked them away, turning them all against the walls, they waited there, unspeakably demanding. There they all were still, all chimeras, chiaroscuro illusions, dead stick figures she had yet to bring to real life, with their umbered pigments upon the canvas ground where formed the limbs the figures the faces of longing, yearning dogs and hungry horses' heads among them, the skulls with ears, liquid porches, spilling light, onto the canvas, pools of it forming into shape of eyes, but as soon as they were formed they ran down with too much turpentine and ran onto the dark dogs and horses, and they turned into echoes of laughter with every mocking sound a different color echoing about the canvas and transfiguring all its painted parts, horses' penises turned to yellow flutes that fitted to manifolds that fitted into female plumbing that in turn dissolved and floated down streets as yellow sunlight, while umbered shadows melted and percolated up into the gutters of tilted houses. If hunger and passion were what was needed for great art, she had it, but it lost itself in the whirl of paint, in the depths of the cave that every canvas became, and the brush could no longer reach it at the boundaries of being. Such was her painting, such was the chaotic state it was in. But she ignored it now, and turned instead to the strike posters her students were working on, and started pulling prints of her own latest design, losing herself in it, until hours later she realized the light was gone in the hugh black-grey cave of the studio, in the high cave that seemed like the inside of a huge black nonobjective painting by Motherwell called *Plato's Cave* or Franz Kline's *Requiem.* She felt herself whirled about and sucked into the grey-black depths of its swirling void, and she went down and out into the dark streets, into the stone labyrinth of the Left Bank in which there seemed to be only darkness and more darkness, and fog in the plane trees, with stick-figure humans disappearing down every street into the endless night that went on and on, as she came finally into the heavy dark of the Place Saint-Sulpice with its strange monstrous church with its monstrous towers, huge in the sky, and its great iron bell like death itself tolling its dark dirge, shaking the heavy buildings, causing dark birds to unroost and flap away into maw of sky. She sat down on a stone bench in the dense dark and looked up at the fleeting fog and the intermittent blurred stars long dead, and the night with no name but hers and Julian's. And just what was she doing, she asked herself, in this Paris in a dumb maze of her own making, in this fog of contradictions? She, a supposedly "dissident" artist, the daughter of old Lefties, what was she doing here now, in love with this rich official of the French banking system who claimed to be some kind of anarchist yet seemed actually to do nothing but go to his bank, eat well, live well, talk revolution, and make love to her? She was living a dream full of moving mirrors, and the fog swirled about her and seemed to grow thicker, some force sweeping her along with it, out of the Place Saint-Sulpice, down another bent stone street into the Rue de Rennes and on down to the Place Saint-Germain and across past its church with stone-twisted apse down the Rue Bonaparte toward the river, buildings and streets merged in a black and white and grey nonobjective landscape down which marched photocopies of dark trees. The perspective she seemed to have lost involved the fragmented figure of Julian, who seemed to flee before her in every distant man she saw, a hawk-like fleeting figure, a fugitive figure which she could never quite see clearly, and she trying to resolve or dissolve this confused painting with the turpentine of reason. It had all reached an unbearable point. The bird that thinks it's escaping its prison flies back at night, hurling itself against its cage, and she came to the river now and turned in his direction, along the Seine, toward where he lived near Chaillot and the Tour Eiffel. She found herself at black midnight at Julian's gate, at his elegant ground-floor flat with its formal garden in back. She stood by the wrought-iron gate and waited for him in the heavy dark. At last he came, looking surprised and pleased. He was in his dressing gown and embraced her and sat her down. "What *is* it, my dear?" He looked in her eyes and took her hand. "It's *you,*" she said. "It's nothing but you! I still—I still don't believe you—believe *in* you. Not at all! It's like I feel you've been filling me with all sorts of wonderful political bullshit." "Really!" said Julian and sat back, as she got in deeper: "Really, and all the while more or less ignoring what's going on in the streets right now, and ignoring what's been happening to me. My students have been putting *me* on the spot these days, instead of the other way around, as I always tried to do, trying to wake them out of *their* deep sleep. . . . So now it's down to this. . . . Either you're with the students or you're against them, there's no middle ground anymore. And I've no way of knowing where *you* really are in all this, where you're really *at*—" "I'm with them, of course," Julian cut in, "and I can see I'm really going to have to prove it. . . ." "How could you be really with them, in your position, with the whole country caught up in it now? You're still a total mystery to me—at least in your daytime life." "I'm glad you added the daytime part at least." She just sat back looking at him, to see him as some stranger would, waiting for his true answers. He got up and paced about and came back to her and began in an intense voice. "I don't mean to play the mystery man with you at all, my dear—and I don't think the gap between me in Lisbon and me here is all that great. In fact, there's no gap at all, as I see it, and I think I see myself pretty clearly." He sat down next to her, and looked away, and began again. "After that time in Paris long ago, I had to go back, back to Lisbon. I was twenty by then, and there was much to be done in Lisbon. Salazar was worse than ever, but we had our little anarchist cells, and my *copains* in those cells were mostly hungrier and more desperate than I. I wanted to stay forever in France but I had to get back to them and what they were doing, or so I thought. I'd made some contacts in Paris. And we were developing our theories— what kind of antifascism were we working for anyway? The reason the state ends up victimizing people is because the state crystallizes all our social conventions— and those conventions themselves are all false—they're not natural laws, they're acquired. Like carrying guns. . . . We are not born carrying guns, we're not born in police uniforms, we're not born wearing gas masks and carrying riot sticks—it's a habit which has grown upon us, so that it almost seems natural, and then it becomes 'natural' to kill each other with guns in the name of law and order and common sense, and so then it becomes perfectly natural for us to kill each other *en masse* periodically, to preserve law and order, to protect our property, our group, our gang, our nation, our tribe, or whatever. Property itself is not something natural we come out of the womb with but it begins to *look* like it's natural, with the laws we set up to pass it on. And so it becomes natural to govern everyone more and more, for the 'greater good,' they say—and Franco becomes natural, Mussolini becomes natural, Salazar becomes natural, Hitler becomes natural. So all this enormous structure we have built up is a social *fiction* which ends up tyrannizing us. And so, either you believe this and you become a real libertarian, or you don't believe it, and you remain a partisan of the bourgeoisie, you remain a *petit bourgeois*—or a *haut bourgeois*. As you said just now, there can't be any middle ground!" "Then how can you be both, on both sides at once, dear Julian?" "Aha! We're coming to that. I wasn't all that naïve, even at twenty—I knew the only way the system could ever be upset would be by a sudden insurrection. But then the same thing would happen again—another gang would take over and make its own new rules, and they in turn would become institutionalized, and there you would have it again, another monstrous organized lie created out of whole cloth, or whole paper, a whole new paper palace, a whole new house of cards, printed with the latest letterheads of those in power. This time it would be *our* gang, but nevertheless, it would end up the same—" Julian stopped short and went to the sideboard and brought back two snifters of cognac. "And that's what will happen," Annie asked stiffly, "to the student revolution now?" Julian snorted: "It won't even get that far! They'll have their 'Czech Spring,' as they're calling it now in Prague, they'll have their little 'summers of love,' their brief euphoric rebellions, full of hope and love and sex, their beautiful little fires of rebellion will burn so bright— and then—pouff—out like a smoking wick with the first winds of winter, the first breath of autumn, the bright leaves will fall to earth, hordes of them, sunburned by *les grandes vacances,* swept away by nothing more than the ticking of the clock, all of them graduated into the real world. . . ." Annie sniffed: "You're very poetic— and very cynical." He sat down again, looking away. Annie took a sketchbook, fiddled with it, took a pen and fiddled with it, unable to speak. She drew angry symbols. Drawing was an addiction with her that went on no matter what. "So, in the meantime," Annie said softly, "in the end you were swept away into a bank?" "Not so fast, not quite so fast. You're forgetting I didn't have all this hindsight then. I still thought it was possible to pass from a fascist society to a really free society without passing through a 'revolutionary dictatorship' of any kind, which then becomes the beginning of another repression, a different drummer with the same old beat." " 'Cynicaler and cynicaler,' said Alice. But so far, it's just a banker's cynicism!" Annie's drawing of him wavered between good and bad, between good and mean and evil. First he looked like a handsome older Dorian Gray, then he looked like Machiavelli. Julian took no notice of her, intent on the fires of his past. "But how," he continued, "how were we to arrive at any enlightened society in a country barely out of the Middle Ages? You should see Lisbon, even today! It's still like some ancient wooden three-masted sailing ship lurching along, listing way over! The whole city's still like some crenellated old decaying castle clinging to its hillsides, an overrun anthill." Julian snorted and sat back again, and went on again. "Well, there were plenty of us. Don't think we were just a handful of isolated intellectuals. No. It was really a workers' movement. And those of us who had some education took care not to confound the goodwill of the workers and their hunger and anger—we took care not to confound that with abstract intellectual talk, 'bullshit' as you say. . . ." "And still," Annie said sweetly, as she drew, "I still want to know how the banker was born out of the student—out of the anarchist, without—without selling out. . . ." "Aha. So you're thinking, probably, that I became a banker and joined the capitalist society because I finally realized anarchism was just an abstract ideal which would never work? If that were the case, then today I'd be just another little functionary in the system! But that's not the case at all—and you're incredulous, of course. Well, I wasn't content just to write and print propaganda and attend meetings. I wanted some kind of forcible insurrection! But that had to be done in such a way that 'liberty' itself wasn't actually destroyed in the process. . . ." Julian paused and got up and paced back and forth again, and his voice took on a sense of reaching some climax. "Yes, well, we're coming to the heart of the matter now. All our underground actions had to be highly organized, with the greatest secrecy, to succeed against the fascist police, who were everywhere. And in the process of organizing underground action, we were—I came to realize—indeed creating a new little tyranny, even though it was a very small one which concerned only ourselves." He paused and sat down again. He stroked her hair absently. *Love!* thought Annie. What a useless word is *love!* Julian went on, oblivious: "Ah, yes—there was the rub—our own little ideal group was far from ideal! We were all sincere, even desperate, and yet we were creating our own tyranny. Some were *naturally* leaders and others followers. And some naturally ended up doing what others said to do. So what was wrong with that if it was indeed 'natural,' if it wasn't the result of repressive conditions? If someone said Go Right here, and another said Go Left, we went in the direction of the one who seemed to know best, et cetera. But the bigger our underground network became, the more power our leaders had over everyone in the underground. So we were creating our own set of controls, claiming they were necessary just temporarily—

just a little temporary exercise of power over the others, for the common good, of course. The trouble is that the supposedly temporary police power never somehow 'withers away' as it is supposed to." Annie had closed her sketchbook and lay back on the couch, her eyes still on his intense face, as he went on and on: "Well, what was I to do then, when I had realized all this and saw it happening? Very simple! Work for the same ends, but work separately! Yes, that was it, that was it exactly. Working separately we'd all be separately free. And acting separately had the advantage of complete secrecy, which we couldn't have in a group. Of course I realized that this could only work during the early stages and that the final 'coup' could only be accomplished by acting together. But we were a long way from that! We were still stuck in the middle. But anyway, when I finally came to these conclusions, I went to my comrades and laid out my new ideas. I was very happy with my argument, for it seemed absolutely clear and true, and I expected them to be happy with it and to agree with me. Well, were they? Of course not! I should have known better. They were too much caught up in their own mythology, or whatever you want to call it. Instead of wringing my hand in agreement, they were very upset with my arguments, which they considered a complete sellout! 'That can't be,' they screamed at me! I argued with them for a long time, for days and days it went on, and not one of them would admit that I was right, that in the end I would be proved right. I saw then that they were really all a bunch of asses, plain and simple, a bunch of donkeys, Sancho Panza's asses who only knew how to follow each other around. A bunch of dumb Spanish asses! They were unmasked now, I saw them all for what they were, little sons and daughters of the eternal poor, the *Lumpenproletariat,* made only for slavery, for continued slavery. They wanted 'liberty' for everyone, in the abstract, but they couldn't give full liberty to anyone to act on his own! Well, I was in an absolute rage. We almost came to blows, three or four of us in the end. I was ready to take them on, all of them. It ended with me just leaving. I just went out and didn't come back. That herd of sheep made me want to throw up. So that was 'human nature,' that's what it had come to! If human nature was really that stupid, then what was the use of any libertarian ideal? But I recovered myself in a few days, after a few days of sulking. If they wouldn't be real anarchists, then I would continue on my own. They wanted just to play at being libertarians, while I considered it more than play. Well, then, how was I to go about it?" Julian stopped and leaned over and stroked her hair again. Somewhere a bell tolled. It was one in the morning. "I'm about to wither away," said Annie. "With hunger! What've you got to eat besides fancy words?" She got up, and they went into the kitchen and opened the refrigerator. "Ah, for some good old American scrambled—" "I've got some," said Julian, "if you can make them American simply by scrambling them." She did, while he followed her around, continuing his story. "Yes, then, what was I going to do? Well, luckily, casting about for some way to proceed on my own, to get *into* the system somehow and attack it on my own, I thought of an ancient friend of my father, a man in his late sixties at least, who nevertheless, I found out, still maintained his position in one of the big banks in Lisbon, in fact in the most important bank of all. What could be better, I thought, if I could somehow get started there, banks being at the very center of everything? Once inside the big evil, I could work to destroy it! Well, to shorten the story, this old friend of my father indeed remembered me as a little boy, when I phoned him, and he immediately invited me to come in and see him, which I did. He hadn't seen me since I was a small child and he exclaimed over my transformation into what he considered a 'handsome young man,' embracing me cordially and offering me a cigar, in the classic style, which I accepted, considering that perhaps smoking cigars with great style was a requisite for any advancement in the banking field. Well, he did indeed find me a position after a while, working under him in fact, as a sort of personal flunky, beginning with the most menial tasks around his office. And I set to work with all my energy to make a success of it, taking on all kinds of personal chores for the master and learning a good deal that I wouldn't ordinarily have had occasion to learn. The job was a stroke of luck indeed, and I stuck to it for seven years, in the same lowly but curiously important position, and I became party to all sorts of confidential information, about how banks are *really* run. . . . But anyway, *tout à coup,* one day the old man, the old gentleman just didn't wake up one morning. There I was sitting in his office one Monday morning, waiting for him to show up, when the word came, and along with it a sealed envelope to his immediate subordinates and to those at the very top of the bank, leaving specific instructions and recommendations that I be eventually promoted to take over a certain important corner of his duties, his most important ones, it seemed, for he evidently had planned very carefully his withdrawal from the world. And thus was I to be the main beneficiary of his whole career! Which may strike you as really unbelievable, except for one fact which I didn't discover until I came by accident some time later upon a little packet of personal letters he had stashed away in the bottom of a cabinet. They were from my own mother! It seemed he had had a long and unrequited love affair with her before she had ever been married, when they were both still in school, or rather while he was still in college and she still in school, for he was quite a bit older than she. In fact, that alone seems to have been the stumbling block that prevented them from ever coming together, for the families were against it from the start. Anyway, thus I was the lucky inheritor of his passions, although he had never breathed a hint about the root of the whole situation. So there I was, still in my late twenties and the heir to a considerable sum of hard cash, even though most of his money went to distant relatives. He had married finally but was a widower by the time I came along. The little nest egg he left me was more money than I had ever dreamed of having all at once. So that was the real beginning of it, the beginning of my real fortune, for I was astute, he hadn't picked me out for nothing. I had a natural aptitude for figures and calculations of all sorts, and after that I didn't waste much time on anything but the manipulation of money and more money and still more money—" "And I suppose," said Annie, eating eggs and ham, "you used nothing but pure anarchist principles and practices to attain your filthy capitalist ends?" "Not at all, not at all, my dear Annie, not for one minute! I was out to beat the evil system, as I conceived it, with all its dirty practices, and I should quibble about my methods? I was working toward freedom from the whole wicked mess, and I should be more critical as to what arms I use to attack? The idiot anarchist with his spiteful little bombs in the street firing at random knows damn well he's going to kill people even though his anarchist theories exclude capital punishment. He's violating his principles but he's right morally because he expects his violent act will make the future better, and I wanted to beat repression and poverty and establish a perfect state, and for that I used any means I could get hold of, without of course creating any *new* evils. Well, I freed myself from the system, by grasping the root of it, money! Having conquered the root of evil, I freed myself—" "Freed *yourself?*" interposed Annie. "But what about everyone *else* still hung up in it?" "Exactly!" said Julian. "And *now* I'm working on that—I can't exactly tell you what I'm up to, right now—" He stopped short and looked in her eyes as they sat down again in the front room. She looked back at him steadily. "Why not?" she asked evenly. He was still looking away. What good was "love," Annie was thinking, in times like this? "Annie, there's so much I'd *like* to tell you right now, about what I'm *really* up to—" Julian fell silent for a moment, then went on in a quieter voice. "You think it's the same old story, don't you? The young revolutionary joins the establishment, with the aim of overthrowing it, like the hero of so many novels, but by the time he arrives at any position of power he's already the victim of it, the victim of all the little compromises or all the big compromises he's made to reach that point, he's already compromised so much that he's part and parcel of the big evil monster. And so dies another brave little revolution!" Annie lay back on the couch and closed her eyes as his voice went on. Everything he was saying made perfect sense. Everything he was saying made no sense at all. He could use words, she was thinking, the way she could use paint, to say anything, to make up any perspective, to construct every kind of illusion, to construct any kind of pleasing picture, true or false. The words flowed like paint, carrying her off with them, over an abstract landscape, in which all that remained was the sound of his voice, the low sound of his voice, which at once lulled and aroused her, as she lay there cut adrift from the sense of his words. It engulfed her like a high tide on a beach where she lay unable to move as the waters came up. It was too late to do anything about it, she could only move with the tide of it, she could only be swept along now, incapable of grasping the shores. What wild higher tides might take them she could never tell, nor control, she had lost control somewhere and could only go with it now, even as she told herself *love* is a useless word, love is a very useless thing. After a long while she heard his voice no more but felt his body upon her, and they lay there like that for a long while, with the dawn coming, and they made love in the first light, and slept the sleep of the living.

▪ 13 ▫

In her sleep she dreamt in French and English or English-French or French-English or confused cutups of the two, a mélange of what was happening in the "outside" world. She was in a café somewhere, they were in a café somewhere, and Julian was saying, "This is the *real* world, this is the way things are," and then he would get up and disappear and come back bearing a chalice of some kind in which there was some kind of potent pure feeling and he would say again, "Yes, this is the way things really are in the real world," and she would drink from the cup of pure feeling as if she had not drunk such a pure draught in many a year, as if she had let pure reason parch her emotions for too long, while he kept saying "drink, drink" in a parody of himself, while words in two languages poured across

the insides of her closed eyelids as if they were little
movie screens, and someone singing "L'Année Folle"

and someone bearing a white phallus
through the wood of the world
looking for a place to surrender it
in *Rêve & révolution*
someone
dragging the earth with
a very small pocketcomb
et *sous les pavés la plage!*
or a horserake such as
farmers
draw across fields
combing the long hair
like an extra in a grade B movie
un témoin passionné
trapped in a celluloid sequence
she could not walk out of it
having no voice of her own
the reel winding onward
with her stuck in it to
the end
un témoin passionné de
ces folles semaines
in a kind of Piblokto madness
in a mistral wind
une crise de civilisation,
disait André Malraux
une crise de croissance
trapped in the celluloid sequence
hypocrite lecteur!
players in an illuminated landscape
a Philistine's tears are

dans une société qui
                    ne se rendait pas comte que . . .
           "The general will against the will of
                              the General"
             que ses vêtements ne lui allaient plus . . .
the paint dripping
              running down abstract
                     over the figura-
                                tive
          dans une crise
                       de conscience
                                 ah
                                      oui
        l'Esprit Quarante-huitard
              and those who make a revolution by halves
                         dig their own graves
          dans les nuits chaudes du
                            quartier latin
                                    ah oui
                   les anarchistes, les marxistes les . . .
    . Now it's beginning to look
                         like it's cracking—
             Be a realist—demand
                        the impossible!
                                  Prenons
                nos désirs
                        pour la réalité
       and the young of frail hands and troubled minds
                 those evicted from the sleep castle
                        only half awake and stirring
                 from now on in the streets shouting
                          naked words and wishes
                  "Il est interdit d'interdire"
                     carrying a white phallus through

                              the wood of the world
        avec une émotion séduisante . . .
                              dictionnaire révolutionaire
                              sème à tout vent. . . .

et je rôdais je flânais je planais en ce temps-là the gardens the masks the Alhambra gardens her open blouse *les blousons noirs drapeaux noirs* days and nights run into each other away awast alone in the far country *si ardente et si folle* on a far strand long ago *dans la rue Mouffetard au crépuscule où je trouvais mon adolescence encore,* and so lie down in a fair field in a far place far ago away alone a last a love along the riverrun to find him there at last in the deep wood where he would come or would not come in the far end of a far day. . . .

▪ 14 ▫

It was the month of May, but hardly the Merry Month of May, as one flabby famous American novelist later called it, for rage wasn't merriment, even in translation, and it wasn't 1789 and it wasn't 1793 and it wasn't 1848, nor 1871, but the first paving stone had been thrown, in the Place Maubert, and the first barricade thrown up, in the Rue Gay-Lussac, and a handwritten sign hung on the door of the amphitheater of the Sorbonne occupied by thousands of students:

THE REVOLUTION

WHICH IS BEGINNING

WILL PUT ON TRIAL

NOT ONLY CAPITALIST SOCIETY

BUT INDUSTRIAL SOCIETY

THE CONSUMER SOCIETY MUST DIE
A VIOLENT DEATH
THE SOCIETY OF ALIENATION
MUST DISAPPEAR FROM HISTORY
WE ARE INVENTING
A NEW ORIGINAL WORLD
POWER TO THE IMAGINATION!

Inside the amphitheater debates were raging twenty-four hours a day, an open tribunal with everyone given the floor, no matter who, from the extreme Right to the extreme Left, militant students demanding democratization of the university and militant nonstudents demanding democratization of *everything* in society, especially the workplace, so that the amphitheater was becoming what one handbill called "the brain of the cultural revolution," addressed by Jean-Paul Sartre for an hour and a half, and by seventy-three-year-old Jean Rostand, who was patron of a movement called Jeune Pouvoir that was "against a regime which offered its young neither a future nor liberty." The hall rocked with Trotskyites, Maoists, anarchists, Situationists, with the statue of Victor Hugo draped in red-and-black anarchist flags, and graffiti quotations everywhere from Lenin, Bakunin, Proudhon, Trotsky, Fourier, Einstein, and Che Guevara. Every day the crowd in the amphitheater increased, one paper reporting "10,000 for 5,000 seats." The Sorbonne had become a free commune with handbills and new journals like *Le Pavé* and *Les Revoltés* and *Le Libertaire*. For the spirit of 'sixty-eight had burst into flame when the rector of the University of Paris called in the riot police to clear the amphitheater, and from that center and from the Nanterre campus in widening circles the fire spread, the revolt spread like a crown fire in a forest, jumping across political lines and boundaries, across class lines and academic distinctions. It was at heart a libertarian revolt of the young, a youth revolt against boring society in general, a global revolt against what they saw as the false values of their elders with their entrenched hierarchies and hereditary authorities backed up by the state and its whole apparatus of control, so that there was a solidarity based not only on youth but on alienation in general, alienation from a fat society that offered its youth no way to enter it. From the university to the factory the "dictatorship of adults" was to be called violently into question, contested at every point, brought to the fire, a contagious and explosive fire that the shock troops of de Gaulle at first knew not how to handle, since they were in fact confronted with the sons and daughters of their own *haute bourgeoisie,* who were creating their own "open university" as a model for an "open society" where imagination would reign in place of dismal bureaucracy. The special riot squads charged up the Boule Miche with their klaxons and bullhorns and battle gear and tear gas, attacking the sons and daughters of the bourgeoisie that supported the regime. This was the fuse that set off "the days of rage," with thirty thousand in the barricaded smoking streets by the fifth of May. For the first time the militants crossed the Seine to the Right Bank and marched up the Champs Elysées, chanting the "Internationale," for there was not a more stirring song in anyone's memory except "La Marseillaise," which had not been picked up by the students because it was "too French" for the French *enragés.* And the difference between the French students' revolt and other revolts that leapt around the world in 'sixty-eight was that theirs was not just a rebellion against a repressive system. For some of them it was also a revolt against "Frenchness," the whole boatload of oversensitive, overrefined, neurotic French intellectual upper-bourgeois culture, effete to the point of decadence, which led one expatriate French poet named Claude Pelieu to call all France "un grand Camembert pourri," a big rotten cheese, with the crenellated battlements of the old regime and its culture like the overripe crust of an old Camembert ready to crumble away, while General de Gaulle told his frightened, hurriedly assembled ministers, "One must act at once! A riot is like a flash fire. . . . You have to smother it in the first few minutes!" But it was too late, almost, for the riots had spread across the country, from university to university, from school to school: Grenoble, Bordeaux, Strasbourg, Aix-en-Provence, Montpellier, while the newspapers began screaming headlines about "The Night of Liberty" and "The Night of the Barricades" and "The Red Night," while now other forces were on the march. A general strike had been called by the unions, the *syndicats,* the blue-collar workers, railroad workers and postal workers, restaurant workers and street sweepers and scavengers. On the thirteenth of May the general strike hit the city, with tens of thousands of students marching arm in arm with workers to the Place de la République, and if the Bastille had still been standing it would have been taken again, for now Paris was burning, the sweet, acrid smell of tear gas everywhere, scenes of desolation up and down the boulevards like battle scenes in the Liberation of Paris 1945, troops of helmeted police charging the massed demonstrators behind barricades of flaming cars. And at the end of the second week in May there was a great march to occupy the Theater of France at the Odéon, with famous poets, playwrights, professors, and editors side by side marching with the students up from the Métro Odéon, where they had met underground; so then at the Odéon another revolutionary free commune sprang into existence with day-and-night sessions on every conceivable subject from dope to free sex to de Gaulle and back again. But, elsewhere, what the Marxists called "recuperation" had already set in, with the unions already stealing the ball away from the original student movement, and the Communist Party beginning to play its opportunist and reactionary role, preventing any real revolution by supporting existing organizations and law-and-order, as it did in every incipient revolution around the world in the sixties. This revolution would be *confiscated* from the students, as happened at the Renault plant, to which the students marched only to find that the unions had locked them out, and the communist unions especially distanced themselves more and more from the students, for the CP hated them because old fart Marx and his ideas had been severely rejected by the student movement, which was anarchist and Trotskyist and visionary, and the CP never really understood the students at all, for their romanticism was closer to Jean-Jacques Rousseau than to Marx. Still the Odéon held out as the ongoing symbol of the original spirit of 'sixty-eight, the *agora,* the people's tribune where the new young spirit spoke and sang. And France would never be the same again, after that flaming month during which half a million people passed through the Odéon's tribune hung with red and black flags under which the most different consciousnesses came together, from the brother of a future President of the Republic to Daniel Cohn-Bendit and Rudy the Red and Jean Genet and Eugene Ionesco and Louis Gilloux and Leo Ferré and John Gerassi and Richard Wright's daughter and Frantz Fanon's daughter and Jean-Jacques Lebel and Herbert Marcuse and Julian Beck and Judith Malina and the Living Theatre. (And where was the voice of André Malraux, that great revolutionary?) While Jean-Louis Barrault, the great mime and director of the Theater of the Odéon, came out on stage, at eleven P.M. on the fifteenth of May, and told Daniel Cohn-Bendit, "I am no longer director of the Theater of France, I am no longer anything but an actor, like all the others. Barrault is dead." And Madeleine Renaud, the great actress and codirector of the theater, addressed the students and said, "I approve of your movement, but why occupy the Odéon? Our theater isn't bourgeois! We've played Ionesco, Beckett, and Adamov!" (In vain! They voted "permanent occupation.") And there were the merely curious mixed with the truly illuminated, all listening or shouting or making speeches, including an astrologer who spouted his prophecies for the year 2000 in the form of quatrains, and a firebug who proposed setting the theater on fire to rekindle the debate, as well as followers of various far-out sects chanting mantras and incantations. Then one day in the middle of a speech by the distinguished brother of a future President of the Republic, a long-haired woman sprang upon the stage, crying, "Comrades, the Bourse is burning!" And they asked the distinguished Olivier Giscard d'Estaing what he thought of that, and he said, "If they have set fire to the symbol of money, I'm with you, but if it's the official collector of the country's money that's being set on fire, then I say No!" "Speak on, oh bourgeois comrade!" someone called out, and they let him continue. But the mob fell out into the streets and paraded toward the Bourse, across the river, and Annie found herself in the middle of a group of International Situationists marching under the banner of philosopher Henri LeFebvre, who had planted early seeds of revolt among his students in Strasbourg

with his manifesto on the misery of student life, his utopian socialism coming long after Charles Fourier among
the strands woven into the present revolt, so that Annie
found herself carried along, if not carried away, by their
euphoria, until all of a sudden, near the Tour Saint-Jacques
just after they had crossed the Seine, she felt herself being
pushed from behind, then felt herself falling in the rush
of a squad of riot police in black helmets, one of whom
jabbed at her with his long truncheon as he swept by,
and she fell back and felt someone catch her, and saw
that it was Julian.

▪ 15 □

"**Y**ou'll get yourself killed, playing Charlotte Corday!" Julian yelled at her, dragging her off the sidewalk and into the little park by the Tour Saint-Jacques, where he sat her down on a bench in the gathering darkness, straightening her blouse and the white scarf she had been wearing for a Leo Ferré concert that afternoon. He dabbed at a big bruise on her left hand with his handkerchief. "That'll teach you," he went on. "Those goons mean business, my dear." "And that'll teach *you*," she retorted. "You'll ruin all your fine hankies, hanging out with me." "And who thinks she's Rosa Luxemburg or Emma Goldman or someone!" he snorted. Which made her laugh as she wiped her face with his handkerchief. "My father had an affair with Emma Goldman once—when she was already quite old." "That's

revolution for you," said Julian. They gathered themselves up and went back across the river, toward her
place, past the Place Saint-Michel, which was suddenly
quite deserted, although the smell of burning rubber
and tear gas hung in the air, the pavement strewn with
broken bottles, scattered barricades, and trash. In the
sky over the Right Bank now there were distant flashes
and dull explosions. A little further on along the quay,
by the Rue de la Bûcherie, George Whitman's Shake-
speare & Company bookstore had been closed for a brief
time, but free events and poetry readings and speeches
by passing American radicals like Stokeley Carmichael
and Bruce Franklin were happening again, sometimes
behind closed shutters, and upstairs now the windows
were wide open and the rooms brightly lit, even though
there had been street fighting right in front that evening.
There were people in the windows, leaning out and
talking and laughing, and the American expatriate bib-
liophile George Whitman with his wild hair and goatee
was rushing about thrusting glasses of tea or punch and
cups of hot soup into strangers' hands, as if they were
survivors from a war, or as if he had his own little expatriate revolution going on here and the rest of the
world only existed when it arrived at his doors. Annie
and Julian had their own world and they passed on along
the quay, Annie limping a little. "And what were *you*
doing there tonight, anyway?" she asked him finally. She
still felt shook up, in a state of shock. There were tears
in her jeans, and she felt sore in the ribs where the
truncheon had struck her. "Well," said Julian, looking a
bit sheepish, "I must admit I was following you—I was
coming over to see you, in fact, hoping to catch you in,
although your phone hadn't answered, and I was just
crossing the Pont au Change when I was astounded to

spot you in the middle of that group with the crazy banners, and I turned around and was just catching up to you when it happened. No one seemed to see what was happening. A bunch of goon police charged in from the quay behind you and were bearing down on the paraders, waving their truncheons and blowing their whistles. At first I thought their whistles were the birds screaming in the little bird market not far away on the quay, I thought they'd just all gone crazy all of a sudden, frightened by the confusion. But birds can't scream like that! I thought. By then I was running too, and then I caught up with you just as that big brave goon got to you." They were heading slowly toward her place, past the Place Maubert, where there was an eerie quiet now, like a battlefield deserted, with the acrid smell of tear gas still heavy in the air. Annie noticed for the first time how Julian was dressed that evening, with an old beret and old grey flannels. He could have been a Harvard professor on sabbatical. "Is this your disguise for the revolution?" "Le Duc de Guise qui se déguise . . ." he quoted. "And, by the way, the Bourse itself wasn't burning, it was just a phone booth set on fire. . . . But, Annie, seriously, what good do you think all that's going to do? Even if they'd succeeded in torching the whole damn Bourse, do you think that would have destroyed the heart of the whole system, or even all its money and papers, most of which has long ago been stashed in safer places? In fact, I'm working on that—" He stopped short, as if he had already said too much. "What?" said Annie, looking in his grey eyes. Julian looked away, and remained silent. And Annie shrugged and looked away too, and there was nothing but silence between them. Annie was angrier than she liked to admit. How could she be so in love with such a hypocrite? Finally she burst out: "According to your so-called anarchist principles, isn't this the famous time of insurrection you're always talking about, the exact moment you've finally got to act, the very moment you've been waiting for? Isn't this *the* moment when you'll finally have to give up 'acting alone' and act with everyone else to bring about the real takeover?" Julian still remained silent, seeming, for the first time since she had known him, very unsure of himself. Twice he seemed about to speak but didn't. They had reached the tiny triangular *place* in front of the Ecole Polytechnique. It too was deserted. The little Café les Pipos was just closing its painted shutters. They sat down on a bench in the dark. If Julian was angry, he didn't show it. It seemed, rather, that a terrible indecision gripped him. He shifted himself on the bench. Two small birds fluttered down from a tree and walked about on the cobblestones, casting long shifting shadows from a streetlight. They had dark markings across the tops of their heads, almost like hats. The one with the heaviest markings seemed to be bullying the other. "He's enforcing his pecking order," Julian observed. "Like just everywhere—the ones with the most braid at the top—the big shots with 'scrambled eggs' on their visors." Annie didn't laugh. It was his same old song. She was waiting for an answer. "Well, Julian?" In chalk on the pavement nearby someone had scrawled "De Gaulle to the Archives!" Finally Julian turned back to Annie. "It *is* the time, and it could really happen this time. It's a much worse crisis than Algeria, for France, for Le Général, and he knows it. The whole greedy structure may be about to tumble! De Gaulle has placed himself above the battle and may go to Baden-Baden to consult with his generals, or to Roumania, he may have left already, who knows, but the whole government is in a state close to chaos!

The National Assembly in emergency session! Half the trains and most of the buses and the Métro aren't running. Workers all across the country are fed up and catching fire. France will *never* be the same! And it'll one day happen all over the world. But I'm *still* going to act alone." He looked at Annie for a long time, and she looked back. Why did people always fink out in the end, Annie was thinking, why didn't they ever come through? Yet, who am I to talk? What have *I* actually done? There was more baffled silence. "Well, Julian, exactly how do you propose to 'act alone,' at this point? And exactly what good will that do at this point?" Still he didn't reply. She was waiting for his words, she was waiting for his answers. How dumb, she was thinking, to love such a man! The little scar on his face seemed to burn. "I *am* going to act alone." Julian turned and looked her in the face. "But—will *you* join me?" She had been waiting for his words. "You mean I've been putting you on the spot all this time, wanting you to put your money where your mouth is, and now here you're putting me on the same spot? What does *that* mean—'Will I join you'?" Julian looked away again, then back at her, and then away again. Again he turned to her, and continued. "I can't tell you much—but you've got to know some—some of it. . . . You know the old Secret Service maxim: only tell the other operatives what they absolutely have to know to carry out their own little part of the plot. . . ." "So it's a plot?" "It's more than that, Anna, it's an actuality, about to happen—in exactly *three days*—the Bank of France is in as much of a panic as the rest. . . . We've activated a certain 'contingency plan.' . . ." "Who is 'we'?" "The blueprint calls for at last moving a very large part of the Bank of France's most valuable stuff to a secret vault out in the country—a top secret location way out of the city.

Paris may actually become an occupied city any day now, by the end of this week the whole country paralyzed, everything at a complete standstill! The general strike has already done that—the whole working population in the whole country will soon be on strike, nobody and nothing working—and Paris perhaps the capital of the *new* 'Free French.' So the Banque de France is taking certain unusual precautions, and I'm the official in charge of the actual transfer! The secret arrangements have already been made, the time and place, the armored cars at the end of a certain ordinary train, and all that, all worked out to the smallest detail, taking into consideration the most outlandish possibilities—except what they'd never suspect—that I have different aims! Everything has been tested. For nothing must go wrong. I can't tell you more—" "And so what do you need me for, window dressing?" Annie felt a certain fluttering in her stomach, if not in her head. "Exactly," Julian said, taking her hand. "That's exactly what you'll be. You'll be my camouflage, dressed like a good bourgeois companion. You'll go to the station with me—to see me off—I won't tell you which station as yet—and I'll be dressed exactly as I am now. I'll be carrying nothing but a little sports bag—an American Spalding bag, such as tennis players carry—and you'll just carry a big briefcase for me—not all that big, really—" "Full of gold certificates?" "Hardly. All that kind of thing, the billions in securities, will already be in the armored cars in the train. All I am to do is deliver them and get a receipt—a single receipt, an official little release. I can't tell you more, right now—" "So what's so revolutionary or anarchist about all that? It sounds like you're just another lackey trying to save the old system—or you're a double agent of some sort, maybe, for all I know!" Annie gave a bitter little laugh. "Fancy little

Annie from Yonkers going around with Daddy War-
bucks, the double agent for the Bank of France!" Julian
gave her that very dark look of his and did not reply.
They sat on like that on the dark bench in the dark *place*.
There was nothing to do but sit there and think that this
was not really happening, not really happening to them,
not here, not now in the middle of love. After a long
time, Julian said in a low voice, "It's the big briefcase
you're to carry for me, handing it over to me at the last
moment—it's that bag that makes the difference—and
I'll show you the contents before we go to the station,
so there'll be no doubt, no doubt—in your—" "And
what's—what's to be in this big briefcase, exactly? Exactly what—" "One very powerful plastic bomb."

▪ 16 ▫

In her waking next morning, the angel of *arrière-pensée* visited her, the black angel, trailing black rags of ulterior motives and afterthoughts. It was a battle with the angel, and on one side was Julian, draped in black flags upon which were inscribed in medieval lettering the double agents of words full of doubt and disillusion. And she, pure white, of course, on the other side, beating off those black harbingers, as if they were death itself, or the death of love at least. She believed in him because she loved him, he was to be trusted because of what he was to her, he was no fraud, no phony. She beat off the black flags of doubt and death. He was using her but he was not using her against her will, for she wished to be used, desired to be used in such a way. She believed in "revolution" too, although it might not be his kind of revolution she wished for, and words he used like *proletariat* and *class struggle* were so outmoded these days, dead terms from another age that really was dying. All the old rads still went around mouthing those famous words as if they still applied! But there was a new focus, with sights raised to a new visionary world view, a cosmic view really, for the spirit of 'sixty-eight around the world wasn't just the tired old Marxist rhetoric warmed over, nor just the old anarchist ideals. It was the first articulation, the first bursting forth of a new vision of earth, of man and woman. It was a new consciousness, or an ancient consciousness rediscovered. And it was a new feminist consciousness, the Gaia hypothesis, based on what was being called the New Physics, the earth seen as Mother Earth again, ancient source of all, and man raping that mother, beginning with Blake's "dark, satanic mills" and roaring forward to the dark, atomic mills, the nuclear mills with their undisposable radioactive wastes. This whole new view a part of the rebellion of the sixties everywhere, a kind of "youthquake" against everything artificial and unnatural in modern life, and the French student revolt a part of the general worldwide cry of youth against the dehumanization of the human animal more and more separated from its animal roots, from earth itself, the green earth. The spirit of 'sixty-eight was the first halting cry of what twenty years later would burst forth in a great new political movement, a new green movement, Green Power, which would have little to do with all the old political labels like Marxist, Maoist, communist, Trotskyite, anarchist, Republican, Democrat, or whatever. It would be a whole new ball game, and it would sweep the world. It was a game that Julian could hardly know, even as Annie was only dimly able to articulate it herself.

It would sweep the world, into the twenty-first century. And in her waking in the dark dawn, she was painting out the night with a brush loaded with light, a huge brush loaded with a new pigment made of nothing but light.

▪ 17 □

And there were two nights left, two nights in two lives, in the days of the *enragés*. Those two nights were one, sleeping and waking, and the dawn coming always. There had been more than one woman's smile in his life, more than one man's body on hers, and there had never been this feeling that it would all go on, no matter what, that no matter what happened they would still be together, would still go on somewhere. In the hot nights of that last week in May in Paris, there was that illusion of eternity. Unreal Paris, with its haunted owls in the dawn up under the eaves of the ancient buildings along the Seine. Unreal Paris, where all seemed suspended, waiting, a beleaguered city. Annie could not believe it was herself involved in all this, she, the dreamer, who had never been that *enga-*

gée. She did not have to go through with it, with Julian. She was not Helen in Egypt, she was not a captive, a hostage, bound to do the will of her captor, she could still back out, refuse to go along with him, in his mad scheme, in *their* mad scheme. Yet she it was who had pushed him to it, and if she would not go on with it, he still would, he would go through with it, he would be gone anyway. And time raced on with them, on its blind rails, toward its own blind ends, wherever. "Loving is eternal innocence," some poet had said, "and the only innocence is not to think." It was as if they were already on separate trains, speeding away from each other. The image of a speeding train came to her over and over in sleep. There were always two trains, sometimes rocking on side by side, other times flashing by each other, their separate faces blurred upon the windows, into the night. Then the trains would flash apart, suddenly out in the open, in the wide landscape, rocking through crossroads and villages asleep, lanterns at crossings, figures with arms upraised, waving. Hello, hello! And they would come to a great lake in her sleep, a strange lake with shells like bones upon the beach, where monsters mixed with boats full of roses and young girls in summer dresses. The monsters had paddles and directed the sailless, rudderless boats while the young girls not yet women went on laughing and singing to themselves and trailing their pale hands in the water, in the pale water where almond-white swimmers floated through hordes of fallen autumn leaves. The leaves lay on the surface of the water like small drifting boats, one upon another, brown boats with stems for prows, and a wind came up and blew them scuttling away, across the waters, with all the *jeunes-filles-en-fleur* aboard them, swept finally over the horizon. She would not be swept away, she was no *jeune-*

fille-en-fleur. She was refinding her self, instead. She would refind her self in the dumb mazes. Beyond the shunting trains. Where life still pulsed, where life would still pulse, for the two of them, perhaps a safe house, a safe place they might somehow reach after it was all over, a white island, *une île blanche,* fugitives in an absurd fugitive dream. . . .

■ 18 □

And the dawn coming always, the last dawn then, and it was Paris which was a white island, adrift in a tule fog, so that they rose like swimmers in the white light, and made their way out into it, into waking Paris, in its white fog in which all sound and sight were muffled, including the called cab that seemed to drift to them. But it had all been arranged, even to the old White Russian driver who seemed to know Monsieur Mendes, and took them aboard as if he were Charon come to ferry them over the River Styx, and piloted his old black Citroën along the banks of the river as if they had all the time in the world. They were right on schedule, to the minute, while Paris in the fog in the depths of a mirror receded behind them, as if everything were being sucked backward down a funnel in the fog, as if there were nothing that could stop it, as if no one could do anything about it any longer, there was only one way to go, and that was down the great river. It was a film they were in and someone had started the projector and no one could stop it. Yes, they had plenty of time, they had time to hold each other in the back of the cab, they had time to tell each other what neither of them really believed, that all would work as planned, that they would be together again in another place. The river drifted past in the fog, and they came to a great bridge in the fog and went over it, to the Gare de Lyon, at 7:22 in the morning in the late May of that year. When they reached the Gare de Lyon it loomed above them like some great Victorian ship with fretted vaults and arches, the filigree of its roof lost in the fog, and they got out, and saw the eternal driver tip his hat, and made their way through a great arch into the enormous *salle des pas perdus,* where already great lines were forming for trains that no longer ran very often. But theirs was to run, theirs was to leave right on time, as this particular train always had. There was still time for them to stroll about for a moment, under the great domes and under the clock near the winding elegant stairs that led to that great old restaurant, Le Train Bleu, with its nineteenth-century dream of life. But they had to hurry now, even as if some magnet pulled them and would pull them apart. The train was waiting on its appointed quay, they could see it, and they moved along its quay, along the platform, past the gleaming diesels, along the gleaming Pullmans. They moved as swimmers still, who would go against the current and were swept on with it. They had lost their steps in the *salle des pas perdus,* and there was no finding them again, there was no taking them back, the two of them were not free, they were not free animals, they were chained somehow, and they swam in their chains against the sea, where foghorns blew, and the train was blowing its blind whistle. For it was time to mount that train, it was time for Julian, his moment, and they embraced, standing beside the armored car, the special car with its door open, waiting for him, and all things must change but never the look they exchanged right then, and then he had turned and the guards were checking and rechecking his papers, and then he was aboard, waving at Annie, he was sitting down in his window seat with his sports bag and his briefcase, which Annie had handed to him at the last moment, holding on to it as long as she could, not wanting him to have it; but now the train started up so noiselessly and gathered speed so fast that his window flashed away with him in it, in an instant, as he still waved, and he had said, "Remember I love you," but the very last thing he had said was "Remember L'Aigle Perdu," ah yes, L'Aigle Perdu, the place they were to meet, this side of the Pyrenees, the tiny town or place where she was to wait for him.

■ 19 □

Thus she went, with the ticket Julian had gotten her. He had made the reservation, he had plotted out her life. She had allowed herself to be driven by pure feeling, and now feeling drove on to the end. She was to leave the station platform immediately, go to a rest room in the station, change her clothes in the locked toilet, and leave her unmarked bag behind. This she did. When she stepped out she had her hiking clothes on, with a small back sack such as students wear slung over one shoulder. She was not to return to her flat. She was to board the fast train leaving for Marseille in twenty-five minutes, perhaps the very last train to get out. She had her ticket and her seat reservation. The "Mistral" was waiting, and she boarded at once and took her seat in the first-class compartment, and sat there waiting for the train to move, hoping no one else would enter the compartment. The train did not move, and she sat there waiting, sure that something had happened, that the last train had been held up and would never get out of the station. But then there was the bright sound of children's voices just outside the double doors of the compartment, and in they came, with a Frenchwoman all in black, who pushed open the sliding doors with a bang and shoved a black valise in ahead of her, as the two boys and two girls tumbled in after her and with subdued excitement sat down and bounced up and down on the plush seats, while the woman in black (who was too old to be their mother but had perhaps been asked to look after them on the trip) finally got her valise wedged up into the overhead rack and sat down by the window opposite Annie, arranging herself with great care on the seat, just as a man's smooth voice came over the loudspeakers, announcing elegantly that "Le Mistral, destination Marseille" was about to depart. And, in a matter of seconds, it began to move noiselessly along the platform, silently as if on soft rails. By the time it had cleared the trainyards it was already hurtling along, and within a very few minutes it was almost out of Paris, gliding south as upon air. The children had little packs with clothes stuffed into them, as if they were being sent to visit relatives in the South for a few days, perhaps to get them out of the turmoil of Paris before it was too late, and they chattered like monkeys among themselves but were very well mannered, very controlled in that particular way of children with well-off parents, and Annie wondered what revolution, if any, they would ever have to make or suffer. And the woman in black took out some black knitting and fell to it like a Madame DeFarge, while her eyes kept track of the four

chattering children and watched Annie and kept knitting
while a waiter in black came by and served Annie coffee
and croissants, which the lady in black refused, and they
all watched as Annie ate her croissant and drank her
coffee, as if they had never seen a foreigner do such a
thing before. They obviously had realized that she was
not French, certainly not one of them. The woman in
black was certainly a housewife and a mother out of the
Midi countryside somewhere; dressed as she was in
shapeless black, she was probably a concierge in some
fashionable resort hotel, or perhaps in a provincial *au-
berge* not so fashionable. She had a shopping bag open
at the top with a baguette sticking out, she wore a little
black hat with hatpins in the bun of her hair, she had
black low-heeled shoes, and varicose veins that showed
through her stockings, her ankles were swollen and she
was overweight, probably from sitting all day behind a
caisse in the hotel and eating three large square meals a
day. Yes, thought Annie, she must definitely be a retired
concierge or the *patronne* of some provincial hotel, going
back home after visiting one of her grown daughters,
who might in fact have been one of Annie's students in
Paris, she no doubt shocked by what her daughter had
been doing, what her prize daughter had been up to at
the Sorbonne or at Nanterre this year. Of course she
had said nothing to her daughter about it. It was the
father who was to speak to the daughter about such things,
when she came home for *les grandes vacances* this
summer. Then things would get straightened out, things
would get sorted out. The father would straighten out
the daughter in such matters, politics and such, and there
would be nothing more to be said about it, with the new
term coming on in the fall and the daughter with her
work cut out for her, if she was to graduate in home

economics. For after all, one had to keep one's eye on the realities of the situation, the realities of life for a *jeune fille* in the provinces, and never mind all that talk about freedom and singing Leo Ferré songs and dancing in the streets with every student who happened along without any proper introduction, never mind about all those political ideas they were always trying to put into the heads of the children, as if they needed any such instruction in such matters except from their father. Yes, what had been good for France and for the glory of France would always be good for France, *ah oui,* Le Général was right, he hadn't saved France from the Boche for nothing, he knew where lay the glory of France. And their children must know it too, they must know which side their bread was buttered on, as the train flew south through the fat country, through the lush green fields. Annie looked at her watch over and over, counting the time to the moment when she knew there would be an explosion on another train, on that other train heading south, and the car at the rear of the train to which she had taken Julian would be destroyed by the huge explosion that would send the whole car hurtling off the tracks, its wreckage burning to the ground in a heap of twisted steel, everything consumed in fire, before the salvage trains and fire fighters could arrive. A few charred documents perhaps would be found but the bulk of that car's cargo would be obliterated from the earth, along with all the blood and sweat of those who had earned that hoard, the cold fruit of the great system gone up in flame. If all went as planned, if all went as she believed Julian had planned it. And if there was no hitch whatsoever then Julian himself would escape. Julian himself would have escaped by now, for it was past the time of the explosion. If he was lucky he would be at the other

end of the train by the time the explosion happened. He
would be far from it, although no doubt the whole train
would be derailed. He would be shook up a bit but safe,
for *that* train was not a very fast train. He might be in-
jured a bit but he would be alive, far from the crime.
He would be free to go, free to come to her, in the
South, where she would be waiting, if all had gone as
was planned. For now the time was well past. Then her
train of a sudden braked and came to a dead silent stop.
There was not a sound, not a noise anywhere along
the train, and no announcements, nothing on the loudspeakers. And there they sat, silent, with a sudden hush
fallen on everyone. There they sat for maybe five full
minutes, for no apparent reason, except what she imagined in her head. Then just as suddenly the train started
up again, went into its fast glide, and in moments seemed
to be back up to its former flashing speed again. The
children went back to their well-mannered chattering
and the concierge went on knitting as if nothing had
happened, for as far as Madame was concerned nothing
had happened to disturb her calm, nothing would ever
happen, and she had not stopped knitting even when
the guillotine fell and life came to a halt, she had gone
right on, counting her sheep or whatever, for there would
always be fat sheep to count, and Annie was to meet
Julian in three days at that certain place near the foot-
hills of the Pyrenees, at L'Aigle Perdu, as now the train
flew on, over the shining landscape, nor could birds keep
up with it, for it was a bird itself, half bird and half woman,
flying low over the landscape, flashing its sleek body, a
whistle in its throat, a silver whistle, singing at country
crossings. Then just as quietly as before the train braked
again, the whole train shivered slightly, like a bird gliding down. In another minute it came again to a full stop

and sat there pulsing, without any announcement, without anyone coming through the cars, no conductors or trainmen or police. They just sat there, all of them silent, looking out the windows at the silent cows that stared back, swishing their tails and chewing their cuds, flicking their tails and wiggling their ears as they chewed, shaking off flies, still looking up at the motionless train on its embankment, as the woman in black kept on knitting without looking up and the children fidgeted and giggled and a cow mooed and turned its head and mooed again. Still no one came through, no police, no sound anywhere, in the middle of nowhere, until of a sudden the train tensed and suddenly was moving again, smoothly picking up speed again, until it was flying once more through the fields, where the sun beat down and the wind moved among the new grasses in the spring of that year, through flickering light and shadow. Annie sat there looking out, pondering the painted landscape of her life and Julian's swart uncertain figure in it, the train rocking on, over the hidden rails. She sat there feeling small and scattered in the too bright sunlight, too much daylight, too much white light hitting her eyes as she tried to sleep, closing her eyes against it, turning her head away from the brightness. There was too much brightness, along the river toward Avignon, too bright the light along the river where the train now glided, and she saw all too clearly where her train was taking her, to the destination she herself had assented to, where she had willingly said she would go, as if she had had full freedom to choose otherwise. Indeed she had. Julian had not pressured her. He had merely offered her his way, his destination, offering to make it hers. And she had. She was to meet Julian in three days, in that certain tiny hamlet this side of the Pyrenees, or at least she imagined it a hamlet, or a group of stone houses on a mountain, a rookery, cloud-hidden. He had not told her that much, only that he had lived there once as a boy. From Marseille she was to take a bus west to Montpellier, and from Montpellier a bus farther west, avoiding the larger towns like Béziers and Carcassonne. In a small town called Béderieux, "a comrade called Lemos" would meet her, in the station café, and take her the rest of the way, part of another day's journey, over the plains and toward the mountains. He would know her by her yellow beret and by a little red rosette Julian had given her to wear in her lapel, like those little Legion of Honor rosettes she had seen in the buttonholes of elderly gentlemen or not so very old men who had been in the Resistance or had otherwise fought for *la gloire de France,* which they had equated with freedom. Annie, in the trance of the train's long flight, sleepless in the bright light, fell into a kind of daze of wondering all about the Julian she didn't know, about the Julian behind the red rosette, the Julian of all those years he had merely touched upon, never revealing to her *very* much of himself in the past, so that she had very little but the present Julian to go on, the Julian she could know and hold. And what was that now but a phantom, an idea, an image in her head, or in her heart, whatever *that* was. What was a heart anyway but the unthinking part of oneself, the heart just another pulsing vulva, another involuntary muscle. And the heart "with its reasons" that reason only sometimes comprehends. And the train sweeping on with her, into an unfathomable future, hidden over the horizon, her head back with eyes closed, as if she might somehow see *through* things better that way, see through time itself, screening out the reality of the actual landscape, making up her own movie on the screen of her closed eyes, her own painting, an enormous landscape in Naples yellow upon which she painted pure light. Yes, all painters came down to this, in the end. First a battle with the image, and then, finally, a battle with light itself, a struggle to capture that light, the light a magic dust that the painter could sprinkle on everything—that light hot upon her now, the Midi sun hot upon her, through the train window, and she felt aroused now in that hot sexual light that had aroused so many painters, creating their so hot paintings, their landscapes of light and desire. . . .

▪ 20 ▫

West of Montpellier, the open country begins, rising toward the distant hills and mountains, a straight two-lane highroad winding through vineyards and poplars, the grey stone houses with orange tile roofs. She was on an old country bus now, and the road mounting through sagebrush and red earth and rocky fields, as in the high country of New Mexico, and then tiny hilltop towns like Tuscany, with houses built of flat stones standing out against the flat sky, standing out like monuments against grey heaven, monuments to the people who had built them, lost in the centuries, true statues of themselves, rocky-faced, hard-bitten, rugged, and there were nested hirondelles up under the eaves of the high houses, you could see them in their tiny mud caves, while farther on in the high fields there were hidden wood larks singing, *alouettes lulus,* maddened with light. And were their cries really cries of ecstasy or of despair? In this far country there had also been clouds of locusts darkening the sun, darkening the land, as now the sky swept over with huge dark clouds, strung out to the horizon, and it was a dark land, a black land, color of flint, color of death and darkness, ancient death of peasants bred into the earth, a country in which no one changed except to die. And here against the thunder sky a stark stone church sounded its iron bell, echoing with a dead sound over the hill, a heavy knell, a death knell, but not for him, not for Julian, Annie thought. Ah no, Annie thought, he's well and all manner of thing will be well, here in this land where the thunder will pass and radiant rain will sweep the plain and a wind will silence the cicadas and flowers turn and turn to the sun again. Life will sing again in the hard land where Julian would come, in the land of birds that was his land, his ancient land where he had known the consciousness of birds, as always he spoke of birds, wherever he was. In Paris, he always heard the birds, as he had heard those distant bird-market birds near Saint-Jacques that day she fell on the pavement. Flights of migratory birds now swept over, westward, toward the mountains. Love is like birds, she thought. Only the greatest don't fly away. A mistral wind pushed her onward, past Villeveyrac and on, through wide open country with white horses and black bulls on the range, so different from the American West through which she had once passed on a bus like this, an old bus with broken seats and a phantom driver lost against the sun falling now behind phantom trees, rows of straight poplars leading down, with small stone bridges and a single railroad track winding away, the road now turning into a valley stretched below seen through the screen of trees, great green fields down in the distance, and a single tall cypress growing out of a ruined stone house on a hill-ock, a white horse loose behind it, grazing, and no peo-ple, no people anywhere in sight, among the lengthen-ing shadows. Hope still lay in the west, even as she knew that hope was an American myth, as due west they turned again, toward a new range of low mountains with round peaks like waves, with terraced hills up close, skirting small towns with narrow twisting streets, Saint-Pargoire, Campagnon, Gignac, and on, and an iron bridge over a river, with bathers dressing in the dusk on a rough beach beneath the bridge. They raise their arms and wave, their laughing faces flashing past, disappearing forever into eternity. So on and on, rocking in the old bus, past Fontes and Paulhan, with graffiti, on a plaster wall

FASCISME

    ROYAUISME

        LIBERTAIRE!

Life was still a dream within a dream, the poplars casting their long shadows across the road, alive as human sil-houettes, arms outstretched, waving. But the landscape turning more savage now, rougher toward the moun-tains, under the bent arms of trees outstretched and the long grasses in the wild fields waving under the mistral wind that maddened all in its wake, all life breathing and moving as if toward some consciousness, some rapt awareness of all things and all beings, in the gathering dusk. Still somewhere there were gold sands singing in desert reaches, as her bus rocked on into the death of sun, and she rode on, in that special trance of travelers at dusk, rapt, *hallucinant, onirique.* And still she heard the voice of dumb hope inside herself, the white statues beckoning, the distant singing. . . .

▪ 21 ▫

So thus it was she met Lemos then, in Béderieux the next morning, after a night's turning sleep in a narrow bed in a narrow hotel, by the Café de la Gare, where she was to meet him, and there he stood, very large, in a wide-brimmed leather hat the color of his skin. Then he came toward her with a questioning look, but the signs were clear and he saw her rosette and stepped up, flashing her a dark look, so like Julian, the same head of heavy hair, the same solitary air of being alone, even in company, even in crowds, especially in crowds. He tipped his hat in an old-world fashion, also like Julian, and smiled his own smile, and grasped her hand in his enormous one, for he was indeed a mountain of a man, a veritable Falstaff, or rather, in the Spanish fashion, a man out of Cervantes, some rough contemporary of Don Quixote, from the high plains of Spain or the mountains of Portugal, perhaps the wild terrain near Monsanto and Castelo Branco. But here he was, wherever he came from. "I believe you're Julian's *compañera,*" he said, in a gruff voice, a bit hesitant. "I'm Lemos. First name's Caiero but they call me Lemos." "I am myself," said Annie, as had been arranged, and the passwords were over. He shook her hand again and turned toward the door of the station with her. "No baggage?" he asked. "None at all," she answered. "Good," he said, in a curious accent, which seemed neither French nor Spanish. "I always like women without any baggage." He laughed gruffly and looked in her eyes. Julian's look again, it was uncanny. They left the station. He had an old truck, and she got in beside him with her little sack. He ground the gears and swung around. It was still early morning, and in a few minutes they were out of the town. Westward again. And southwestward. A straight road southwestward, rising slightly, small wild mountains to the west and north. She had never been in this country, never in this deep part of southern France, although she had been as far south as Roc Amador once, on a walking trip by herself. Roc Amador, where nothing relieved a feeling of desolation and loneliness, in a *paysage sauvage* that seemed to have been abandoned and forgotten in some other century, a land "God forgot," as a local maxim had it, almost as if it were Calabria or somewhere lost in Sicily. Roc Amador, somewhere near here perhaps, and here she had the same feeling of loneliness and desolation and abandonment, although she had felt instantly accepted by this huge gruff warm hulk of a man driving the open truck through the rising warmth of that morning. The southern sun was already rising above Béderieux behind them, beginning to warm their backs. The southern sun would soon scorch them, for this was no *morte saison*. Here the late spring breathed with a vengeance, the hot breath of the Van Gogh sun, an almost sexual breathing, as they drove on, silent. Annie looked over at him, at Lemos. She felt a certain attraction to him. She felt a need to speak, for this strange silent hulk held the keys to so much she still wanted to know, to fathom about Julian Mendes. Yes, how very little she actually knew about Julian, after all, after all the nights they had spent together—more nights than days. The day time they had spent together was not that great, and it was as if one thought differently at night, as if one's mind underwent some kind of intangible transformation when the sun went down. With darkness the mind became another animal, a sleeping one, with eyes closed, somnolent, while the rest of one's being continued, pilotless, still required to breathe and act. And night became a shadowed landscape, lush with flesh through which one groped. Day was another land, where all was clear, where all stood out clearly, facts like landmarks standing out, all clear, defined by reason and logic. Here was Lemos, who perhaps could clarify much, if he would. She had assumed that "Lemos" was an old friend of Julian, but he had not told her that much. Perhaps he was just a *compañero* in the movement, in some anarchist underground group, someone Julian had never even actually met in person. Annie looked over at him again, seeing how calmly he drove, almost as if by himself, as if perhaps this were just a job he had to do, like a chauffeur. Yet there was something so similar to Julian in his look, something so deep, so much akin, it was almost as if she loved him too. She knew he must be close to Julian in one way or another, or sometime had been close. Still she remained silent too under the

sun which seemed to speak its own hot language, wordless heat upon the landscape, this landscape that opened
to the sun like a huge sunflower, a sunflower as huge
as the yellow land itself. Still she was not a part of that
hot wordless landscape, as he was; she was on her own
journey, and she had yet to find out what his journey
was, what his trip was, and where he was coming from,
this curiously taciturn man. Suddenly he laughed, and
the whole seat seemed to shake. "The absurdity of it
all!" he exclaimed, turning toward her slightly, as the
truck bounced along the straight road, which had turned
to dirt. "The absolute absurdity of the whole story!" He
spoke French with Spanish *r*'s as they did in that region.
He gave another great laugh. "Imagine," he went on,
"what an idiotic trip we're all on! My old *copain* Julian
and me and the rest—all of us on this insane journey."
His eyes flashed at Annie. "All absurd! To think that the
way we've chosen is any better than any other, . . . Because we're using violence too! Julian's using violence
too—to get to the paradise he has in mind—to get to
his precious eagle's nest, where only peace and love will
reign!" Lemos thumped the old steering wheel of the
truck as he spoke. He let out another huge laugh, seemed
about to speak again, but fell silent, as the truck ground
on. After a while, Annie said, "And just where and what
is this L'Aigle Perdu?" "Aha!" exclaimed Lemos with another great laugh. "We got a good way to go—the last
part by horse. Can you ride?" "Somewhat! The town's
that inaccessible?" "Hardly a town," said Lemos, "a house
by itself, on the mountain, above Cailho, well hidden."
He looked out on the land somberly. "There's been no
word," he said finally. "Nothing in the papers, nothing
on the radio—but I'll take you to a place. . . ." "A kind
of safe house, then?" "*His* house," said Lemos. "We play

there as kids. It was a ruin and we named it L'Aigle Perdu. I was kind of big brother—a cousin, really—on poor French side of family. He bought the house much later— much later—not so long ago—and I been restoring. . . ." Lemos lapsed into silence again, staring at the landscape moodily, and the sun beat down on them in the open truck. Suddenly he burst out again. "All ideologies idiotic, no? Thinking itself idiotic! We start thinking and get ideas and divide everything up into ideas, and the ideas become ideologies, and then the tribes go to war over their ideas, these ideologies which are nothing more than obsessions, obsessions of the tribe! Just like primitive tribes with totems, sticking pins into their totems to kill their enemies!" Lemos was roaring now, with his own obsessions, as if he perhaps hadn't had anyone to talk to in a long while. "Quelle connerie! We're all refugees from violence down here, and it comes from both sides, and the little man caught in the middle as usual, as he always has been. . . ." "Or the little woman." Lemos went on as if she hadn't spoken. The road was getting bumpier, dustier. "Paris—London—Rome—student riots!" he snorted. "Them big tribes with all their rulers and police never succeed in bringing about peace and beauty and love and freedom, so there's this general revolt against authority all over the world and you got all these students running around and the cops beating up on them. . . ." His voice drifted off, his eyes on the road way ahead, as the truck bounced along and the sun beat down. Annie was seeing him anew, a different version of Julian, the other side of Julian. But even his vehement opinions made her feel that Julian was for real. Lemos by his very existence somehow made Annie believe in Julian, in the truth of his life as he had told it to her. Julian and Annie no longer existed in a vacuum, now that she had met this "comrade" who knew and judged Julian and his ideas. "So what then?" Lemos burst forth again, his eyes still on the far road. "So what then, if thought itself is the destroyer—if thought itself divide us up into hate groups and set us killing each other, over and over, century after century—only we're better at it now than ever before—ten thousand wars in five thousand years! And then—where exactly—exactly where—where is what they call 'love' in all this?" He turned to her as if she should have the answer. "Is this so-called 'love' too just another thought, just another product of thinking—that demon thinking which causes all the trouble in the first place? This thing called 'love,' which the politicians and the priests and marriage itself destroy!" Of course there was no answer. She saw him now only as a very lonely man in his open truck as he slowed down now and turned off the main road, onto a single dirt road up the mountain, as the mad sun rose higher behind them. And there was only silence in that sun, as they ground on, more slowly now. After a while Annie said: "So there's nothing left, then, but to go it alone?" "One must be like a bird," said Lemos, and he said no more. He was sweating under his leather hat in the sun, and the sun beat down as they wheeled on, turning and turning up the steep rutted road. " 'Turning and turning in a widening gyre,' " thought Annie, " 'the falcon cannot *see* the falconer. . . .' " And at last they came to little Cailho, and the truck ground in second gear up its steep main street, its only street, deep-rutted, to the tiny village square, which was no more than the space between three stone houses set around a well where an iron bucket hung. Lemos pulled up next to it and stopped, turning off the boiling engine, which shuddered and sank back like an old horse. Lemos sat there in the truck, fanning himself with his big hat. "There's a tale," he said, "of the peasant who buried her husband near this well and still came to hear his voice all the time, down in the well. . . . She heard it whenever she wanted to, she said, he was still there for her. . . ." His voice trailed off. He got out, stretching, putting his leather hat back on. Annie got down and stood under a dead olive tree, looking around at the dozen stone houses up and down the steep silent street of the half-abandoned town with its little stone church at the upper end. There was a silence of centuries on this far place. An atmosphere of sleep and dream. Nothing moved. It was a long time since the drought had killed the olive trees. A worn face or two peered out from upper windows, and she heard voices in the old stone house that Lemos now entered through a door with a bead curtain. After a minute or two or three he came out with his leather hat in his hand. His eyes went over her. "The horses are ready," he said. "Up behind the church." They drank at the well and slowly, then, walked up and found the grey horses tethered in the shade of a huge plane tree, and Lemos put the saddles up and cinched them. She swung up in a moment, looking like an American cowgirl in her jeans, and they turned up the steep street on their mountain horses to where a path led off through chestnut trees at the top of the ruined town. And so set off up the final mountain, toward Julian's rookery, through the ruined orchards and open meadows. Her horse lengthened its stride toward the mountains, finding its own way, sure of its footing, now through brambles on a rocky path upward, descending a gulch and crossing a stream and climbing again, up and up. Somewhere a long way off a train hooted, the far lonely cry of trains. It was as if it were a call-back to reality, a recall to the real world, to the life she had left and was leaving. And a train rocking through her sleep forever now, always leaving a station with its precious cargo, its freighted cargo, and never arriving anywhere, shunting through her sleep and never and never arriving, the shattered siren sound of the train's whistle lost and found in the night and day far off, echoing over the painted landscape always as if it were some shattered echoing dream of life on earth, the somehow never-realized dream of ideal human life, the utopian zero summer. Oh, the love of earth, the terrible longing of physical life, the teeming hunger of life, rooted in earth, yellow flowers bright in green foliage, on the bright hills, in the groin of hills, the sexual soil hot in the sun, antlered trees in the thick earth, and the lowing in loam of earth, the lovers in their moaning, the dancers under the hill laughing and calling, the voices over the river, calling and singing their hunger for living, a wild thirst in the wild earth where all things breathed. And they came out in a high meadow and started across it, in the noon sun, in the Midi sun, among the silk cords of sunlight, the white heat beating down on the hot lush fields full of yellow flowers, Lemos up ahead, hunched over on his little mountain horse, like some lost knight, and Annie following, in a euphoria of sun, the heat upon her, hatless, waves of light whirling down upon her, only herself in the flaming sun, her body hot in the hot grasses, in the burning flesh of the high meadow where Julian would come or would not come with his answers, and she would lie down with animals there, she would lie down in the hot grasses, with the flesh that was one with hers, she felt his lips upon her, in that gold field at the end of time, where all beings breathed as one, where now a line of brilliant birds flew over, high away, the sunlight bright upon them, winging westward, and they swung about as if to seek some opening, some pass in the high mountains, some way to the sea, the open sea somewhere, where seabirds wheeled and cawed and cawed and cawed and cried their unthinking threnodies.